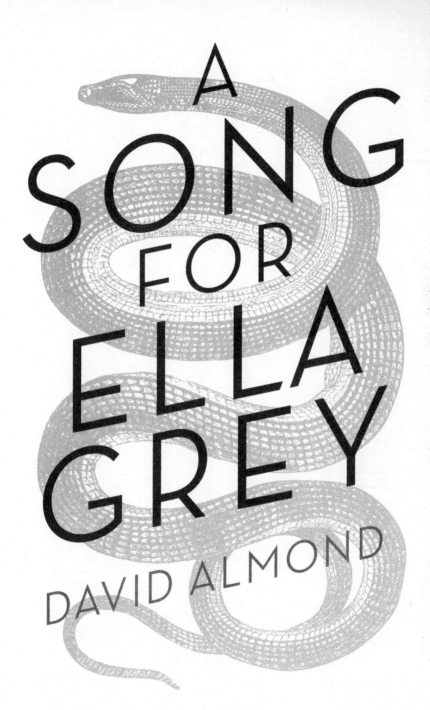

A SONG FOR ELLA GREY

DAVID ALMOND

Delacorte Press

Dear Reader,

This is a new novel, but it tells an ancient tale. It's set in the northern part of the world in which I live today but draws on the Greece of thousands of years ago. Its characters are modern teenagers, but two of them live the lives of doomed lovers from the distant past.

I've always loved the myth of Orpheus and Eurydice. It's a story of love and death, darkness and light, hope and despair. It's a tragedy that is filled with joy.

Orpheus is the greatest singer and poet the world has ever known. When he plays his lyre, the birds come down from the sky to hear him, wild animals are tame, even the trees bow their heads to be near him. He wanders the world, enchanting all who hear him. Among his listeners is beautiful Eurydice. They fall in love with each other; they marry. But a snake bites her as she walks in the garden and she dies. Orpheus is distraught. His music becomes filled with a new dark beauty, with longing for his lost love. He determines that he will find the entrance to the Underworld, that he will go there, the one living thing among all the dead, and bring her back. He does find the entrance. He sings his way into the darkness. He enchants the guardians of the Underworld. He enchants its rulers. He enchants Death itself. Eurydice is called from the depths. Yes, he can lead her back to the upper world. There is just one condition: he must not turn to look at her until they are both in the light again. So he sings his way out of the darkness. Eurydice follows. But just as they are about to reach the world of life and light, he turns, and his Eurydice is taken back.

It's a tale that says much about human love and yearning, about the purpose and beauty of poetry, music and song. It tells of our longing to transcend death, to bring our lost loved ones back to us. And it's a tale of young people, of first passion, first love.

Ella Grey is our Eurydice. Her tragedy is told by Ella's best friend, Claire. She sees Orpheus and Ella grow intoxicated by the love they feel for each other; she records the overwhelming joy and the profound despair they experience. She sees that there seems no way to halt their destined fate.

It was such a powerful book to write. I felt that I'd touched on some very ancient forces. At times, I really did feel that the words I wrote were being sung for me. I hope you enjoy it.

David Almond

FOR FREYA AND HER FRIENDS

Text copyright © 2014 by David Almond
Jacket photograph copyright © 2015 by Ilina Simeonova/Trevillion Images

All rights reserved. Published in the United States by Delacorte Press, an imprint of Random House Children's Books, a division of Penguin Random House LLC, New York. Originally published in hardcover by Hodder Children's Books, London, in 2014.

Delacorte Press is a registered trademark and the colophon is a trademark of Penguin Random House LLC.

Visit us on the Web! randomhouseteens.com

Educators and librarians, for a variety of teaching tools, visit us at RHTeachersLibrarians.com

Library of Congress Cataloging-in-Publication Data
Almond, David.
A song for Ella Grey / David Almond. — First American edition.
pages cm.
"Originally published in hardcover by Hodder Children's Books, London, in 2014."
Summary: Claire witnesses a love so dramatic it is as if Ella Grey has been captured and taken from her, but the loss of her best friend to the arms of Orpheus is nothing compared to the loss she feels when Ella is taken from the world in this modern take on the myth of Orpheus and Eurydice set in Northern England.
ISBN 978-0-553-53359-0 (hardcover) — ISBN 978-0-553-53360-6 (library binding) — ISBN 978-0-553-53361-3 (ebook)
1. Eurydice (Greek mythological character)—Juvenile fiction. 2. Orpheus (Greek mythological character)—Juvenile fiction. [1. Eurydice (Greek mythological character)—Fiction. 2. Orpheus (Greek mythological character)—Fiction. 3. Mythology, Greek—Fiction. 4. Love—Fiction. 5. Friendship—Fiction. 6. England—Fiction.] I. Title.
PZ7.A448Son 2015
[Fic]—dc23
2014040181

Printed in the United States of America
10 9 8 7 6 5 4 3 2 1
First American Edition 2015

PART ONE

I'm the one who's left behind. I'm the one to tell the tale. I knew them both, knew how they lived and how they died. It didn't happen long ago. I'm young, like them. Like *them*? Can that be possible? Can you be both young and dead? I don't have time to think of that. I need to cast the story out and live my life. I'll tell it fast and true to get it gone, right now, while darkness deepens over the icy North and the bitter stars shine down. I'll finish it by morning. I'll bring my friend into the world for one last night then let her go forever. Follow me, one word then another, one sentence then another, one death then another. Don't hesitate. Keep moving forward with me through the night. It won't take long. Don't look back.

I'll start in the middle of it when the wheels were already turning, when the end was still to come. It was a late spring early morning, two weeks into the new term, and we were in bed, the two of us together, as we were so often then. It's how our sleepovers had developed. We started out as five-year-olds cuddled up with teddy bears and fleecy jimjams. Now here we were at seventeen, still spending nights together. They'd been stopped by her parents for a while. They'd said she was too old for this. They'd said she was going astray, not working hard enough at school. But she'd knuckled down as they'd told her to. She'd wrapped them around her finger as only she could. And here we were again, sleeping tucked against each other in my safe warm bed, breathing together, dreaming together. Ella and Claire. Claire and Ella, just as it had always been. So lovely. So young and bright and free and . . . And our futures lay beyond us, waiting. And . . . Ha!

Light filtered through the thin yellow curtains. My dangling wind chime sounded in the draught and the shabby dreamcatcher swayed. A river bell rang on the turning tide and a foghorn groaned far out at sea.

I thought Ella was still asleep. I had my cheek against her back and listened to the steady rhythmic beating of her heart, to the hum of life deep down in her.

"Claire," she softly said. "Are you awake?"

"I thought you were asleep."

"No." She didn't move. "It's love, Claire. I *know* it's love."

My heart quickened.

"What d'you mean, love?"

I heard the smile on her breath, her sigh of joy.

"I've been awake all night," she said, "just thinking of him."

"Him?" I demanded. "Who do you mean, *him?"*

I removed myself from her. I rolled onto my back.

I knew her answer, of course.

"Orpheus!" she whispered. "Orpheus! Who else could it be?"

She giggled. She turned to me and she was shining.

"Claire! I am in love with him."

"But you haven't even *met* him. He hardly even knows you bliddy *exist*."

She went on giggling.

"And you've only spoken to him on the bliddy . . ."

She pressed her finger to my lips.

"None of that matters. I keep on hearing his song. It's like I've been waiting to find him, and for him to find me. It's like I've known him forever. And he's known me."

"Oh, Ella."

"It's destined. I love him and he'll love me. There'll be no other way."

Then my mother's voice, calling us down.

"Coming!" called Ella.

She held my face, gazed into my eyes.

"Thank you," she said.

"For *what*?"

"For bringing us together."

"What?"

"If you hadn't called me that day and told me to listen, and if he hadn't sung to me . . ." She kissed me on the lips. "None of this would have happened, would it?"

Mum called again.

"Claire! Ella!"

I pulled my clothes on.

"No," I said.

She just kept on smiling.

She kissed me again.

"You'll see," she said. "You'll understand. It won't be long now."

"What won't be long?"

"Until he comes for me. I *know* he'll come for me."

She kissed me again.

Thud, went my heart. *Thud.*

• • •

We walked to school along the riverbank, past where the shipyards used to be. We crossed the bridge over the burn where we once sailed paper boats and bathed our dolls. The high arches of the Newcastle bridges shimmered in the distance. We passed some men fishing. Part of the pathway had collapsed into itself, probably into one of the multiple cavities left by ancient mining works.

I took her hand and guided her across.

I took her face in my hands and held it gently.

"You're such a total innocent," I told her. "You've never even had a proper lad before, and now . . ."

She giggled, the way she did.

"It's how it happens, isn't it? One day everything's just ordinary. And then kapow, out of the blue, you fall . . ."

"It can't be love," I said. "It's madness."

"Then let me be mad!"

She kissed me in delight and stepped away and we hurried on. Others were around us now, all making their way to Holy Trinity. We called out greetings to our friends.

She hesitated before the gates and spoke softly, conspiratorially.

"I know you're jealous," she said.

She came in close again, lowered her eyes and whispered soft and low.

"I know you love me, Claire."

"Of course I do. Proper love, not this . . ."

"I'll still be here for you," she said. "I'll still be your . . ."

"Oh, Ella, stop it. Stop it now."

I tried to hold her, but she broke away, didn't look back.

In English that morning, Krakatoa's droning on and on and on and on. *Paradise* damn *Lost* again. I'm watching Ella staring from the window. Always such a dreamer. Sometimes it's like she's hardly there at all. Sometimes it's like she's half-dead and I'm the one doing her living for her.

Sometimes you just want to kick her arse and shake her up and snap,

"Wake up!"

"Claire?" comes Krakatoa's voice.

He's right by my desk.

"Yes, sir?"

"What do *you* think?"

"About what, sir?"

He rolls his eyes, but he can't go on, because suddenly Ella's out of her seat and stuffing her things into her bag.

"Ella?" he says.

She doesn't even look at him. She grins at me. She makes a fist of joy.

"*See?*" she whispers. "Didn't I tell you, Claire?"

And she laughs and she's out the door and gone.

Then we see him, out in the shimmering at the edge of the yard. Just standing there, with the coat and the hair and the lyre strapped to his back, gazing towards us with that Orpheus look. And now there's Ella, hurrying over the concrete to him.

Krakatoa yanks the window open.

"Ella!" he calls. "Ella Grey!"

She doesn't turn. There's a moment when she and Orpheus just stare at each other, seeing each other for the very first time. Then they take each other's hands and off they go.

Krakatoa gives one more yell, then shoves the window shut again.

"Doesn't say boo to a goose and then up she comes with this?" he says. "Who'll ever understand you kids?"

"It was true, then," whispers Angeline at my side.

"Aye," I whisper back.

"She said he'd come, and so he did."

"He did."

"She's the dark one. Who'd have thought it?"

We stare at the space they've left behind.

"Her and *him,*" says Angeline. "Her and *him.*"

There's lots of others at the window.

"Who is he?" says Bianca.

"He's sex on a bliddy stick!" laughs Crystal Carr.

None of the boys says anything.

"Back to your seats," says Krakatoa. "If she wants to throw away her chances then so be it. She's her own person."

"Is she?" I grunt.

"Who *is* he?" says Bianca. "Who?"

"So let's go on," says Krakatoa. "Evil, be thou my good. What exactly does Milton mean by this?"

"Who?" says Crystal.

"He's called Orpheus," I say. "Bliddy Orpheus."

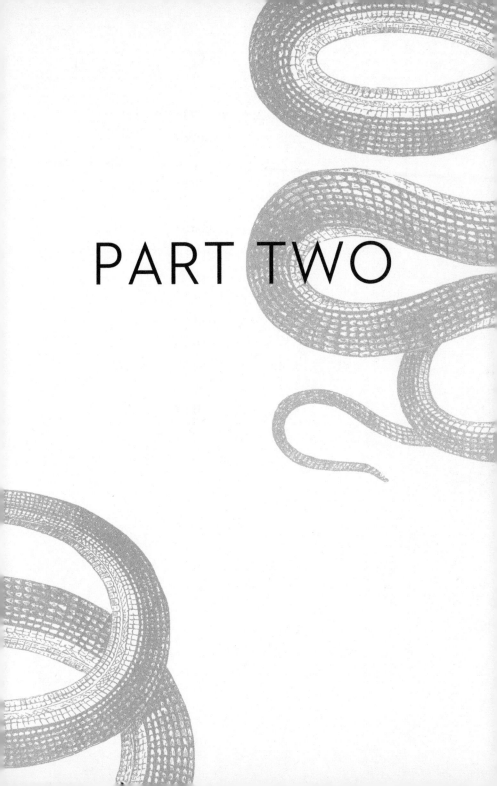

PART TWO

ONE

Maybe he was always with us. Maybe he was there when we were thirteen, fourteen, fifteen, sixteen, when we were forming our beautiful friendship group. We used to meet up on the grassy slope beside The Cluny, that old whisky warehouse converted into artists' workshops. It's down by the Ouseburn, the stream that comes out from under the city then flows through its gates down into the Tyne. There's a café, a bar, a little theatre, a room where bands play. Close by is Seven Stories, the children's book place. When we were little, we used to go there with our parents and teachers to listen to writers and artists. We'd make masks and put on costumes and act out stories of our own. We'd speak through our masks and say, I'm not me. I've gone. I've turned into Dracula, or Cinderella, Hansel, Gretel, Guinevere. And then we'd tell our tales and write them down. And as I write this down, I think that he was with us even then, speaking through us, making us sing, making us dance.

We always said there was magic in the air down by the Ouseburn. We'd sip wine, listen to the river, stare up at the stars, share our dreams of being artists, musicians, poets, wanderers, anything different, anything new. We scoffed at the kids who weren't like us, the ones who already talked about careers, or bliddy mortgages and pensions. Kids wanting to be old before they were young. Kids wanting to be dead before they'd lived. They were digging their own graves, building the walls of their own damn jails. Us, we hung on to our youth. We were footloose, fancy free. We said we'd never grow boring and old. We plundered charity shops for vintage clothes. We bought battered Levis and gorgeous faded velvet stuff from Attica in High Bridge. We wore coloured boots, hemp scarves from Gaia. We read Baudelaire and Byron. We read our poems to each other. We wrote songs and posted them on YouTube. We formed bands. We talked of the amazing journeys we'd take together once school was done. Sometimes we paired off, made couples that lasted for a little while, but the group was us. We hung together. We could say anything to each other. We loved each other.

There was one Saturday dusk when Orpheus was surely in the air. Early spring, but already the temperature had started to rise. Above the city, the sky was pink and gold. The grass we sat on still held some heat from that day's sun. From the quayside, further in towards the city, came the laughter and screams of early drunks. Somebody had brought a bottle of Tesco Valpolicella and we were passing it round, mouth to mouth, tasting each other as we tasted the wine.

We all gasped at the dark silhouette of a single swan that swooped towards us from the metro bridge high above. It swerved just a few feet over our heads, and rushed towards the river. We cursed with joy. We applauded, laughed, smiled, sighed our way into the stillness afterwards.

I was leaning back with my legs stretched. Ella was leaning back on me. It was she who heard it first.

"What the hell is *that*?" she suddenly said.

"Is *what*?"

"Is *that*?"

She sat up straight.

"*That*. Listen."

What was it? We listened. We heard nothing, then we did.

"There is *something*," said Sam Hinds.

"That kind of singing or something?" said Angeline.

"Aye," said Ella. "That."

Aye, like singing. But also like a mixup of the river sounds, the drunks, the air on our faces, bits of birdsong and traffic, like all of those familiar things but with a new note in them that turned it all to some kind of weird song.

We listened hard.

"Naah," said Michael. "It's nowt."

But it wasn't nowt. Otherwise why would we all get up like we did and start searching for its source? Why did we all say that yes, we could hear it? Or is that just how we were then, ready to find weirdness and beauty where they didn't really exist? Was it just the Valpolicella and the swan and us being together and being young and being daft?

Whatever it was, we got up. I swigged the last of the wine and chucked the bottle into a bin. We went down the grassy bank to the Ouseburn, which flowed through the deep shadow cast by The Cluny. Water, spinning and spiralling and gurgling as it flowed down to its meeting with the Tyne. The slick black glossy mud at the edge clicking as it dried. Footsteps of a couple as they crossed the narrow steel bridge over it. I held Ella's hand as we walked.

We followed the stream to where it emerged from its tunnel beneath the city. It gushed through the metal bars of locked gates. We gazed at the bolts and massive padlocks, the rusted warning sign with the skull-and-crossbones on it, the arched tunnel beyond, the deepening darkness.

"God, how scary this used to be!" she said.

"Remember staring in, peeling our eyes to see who could see furthest?"

"Seeing all those fiends and monsters?"

"And all those rats that slithered out that time?"

"And running away yelling and screaming?"

We giggled.

"There's one!" I said.

"And another, Claire! Look! The one with horns! Oh no!"

We were joking but we trembled. I drew her to me and kissed her full on the lips. It was in just this place that I had done this first, those years ago when we were still those infants scared by the dark.

"Listen," she said. "It's like it's in the water, Claire. Can you hear?"

We listened to the way it flowed through the gates, between the banks.

"Aye!" I said.

We laughed.

"Tinkle tinkle," I said.

"Gush gush gush!"

But then the sound we searched for seemed to come from everywhere. We walked away from the water. It came from a different direction at every corner, from a different place each time we paused.

"Where *is* it coming from?" I said.

Ella closed her eyes and turned her face to the sky.

"From inside us!" she said.

Carlo Brooks, who looked the oldest of us, went into The Cluny bar to get more wine. We swigged it and we walked on, not searching now, just wandering through the sound. Maria and Michael, who'd been teasing each other for weeks, slid into a doorway, held each other, and started to kiss passionately at last.

"Yes, go on," called Catherine. "Love each other now!"

A group of drunken lasses swaggered past us.

"It's the hipster crew!" they laughed.

We giggled when they'd gone.

"Hipsters!" we scoffed.

"That's us!" laughed Sam.

We kept on listening. Did it fade or did we just stop hearing it—or was it never really there at all? Who knows? Anyway, we realized it was gone. We came to the quayside. We walked by the bars and the restaurants, through gangs of drinkers.

There was a busker under the Tyne Bridge, an old bloke with a lined filthy face playing a battered mandolin and singing something foreign in a croaky voice.

"Mebbe it was just him all the time," said Sam.

We stood and listened for a moment.

"He must have been lovely at one time," said Ella.

The bloke gestured down to the old mandolin case on the ground at his feet.

We found a few coins, threw them in.

He smiled at us and held his mandolin towards the sky.

"The Gods will reward ye," he said, and he played again with new verve.

"Wow!" said Carlo. "How good would you get if we threw some tenners in?"

The bloke laughed.

"Give me your everything," he said. "And you will see."

I walked homeward with silent Ella.

"Maybe it was nothing," she said. "Maybe it *was* just something coming out of us."

I left her at her gate. She hardly moved. She stepped back, stared at me like it wasn't me she was staring at.

"It's mad," she said.

"What is?"

"Being us, being young! It's amazing! Isn't it, Claire? *Isn't* it? Say yes! Say *yes!*"

"Yes," I whispered.

And she giggled, shrugged, turned, was gone.

TWO

Next day we discovered that some of us had gone on hearing it, in our sleep, in our dreams. Not me. Their eyes widened and they gasped as they realized they weren't the only ones. They said they wanted to hear it again, find it again.

In English, Ella was off with the fairies again.

"So," said Krakatoa. "'Twice or thrice had I loved thee, Before I knew thy face or name.'" What are your thoughts about this, Miss Grey? *Miss Grey! Your thoughts!*"

I elbowed her awake.

"I think," she said, "it is really beautiful."

"Yes. And?"

"And . . . weird, sir. Like sort of dead mysterious."

"Ah, the Beautiful, Weird and Like Sort of Dead Mysterious School of Criticism. Excellent." His face darkened. "Sadly, this is not a school acknowledged by your A Level examiners. Miss Finch?"

Bianca jumped.

"Me?"

"Yes, you, Miss Finch. What do you think our Mr. Donne is on about."

Bianca drew a file across her nails for a moment as she pondered Krakatoa's face.

"Well, sir," she said. "I think Mr. Donne is saying that he's gagging for a good shag."

She paused. Krakatoa didn't flinch.

"To be honest," she continued, "I think that's what them poets is always on about."

She contemplated him.

"Or mebbe you don't get that sort of thing, sir."

We watched the face of Krakatoa. Was this to be an eruption day?

No. Not this day.

THREE

Back then, exams were approaching, the walls of the system were closing in. Ella's parents said they were deeply concerned about her attitude. She'd been such a clever girl but was rapidly turning into a silly dreamer. She was squandering everything. Her reports were extremely disappointing and her anticipated grades were in steep decline. Didn't she *want* to have good results? Didn't she *want* to get to a good university? Didn't she *want* a successful life?

"What do they mean, a successful life?" I said.

"Money and stuff, I suppose."

"Money and stuff?"

"And a good job and all that stuff."

I imagined how vague she'd be with them, how she wouldn't stand up for herself, how she'd just shrug and um and err and shut her eyes, and tell them she was sorry and she'd get better and try harder.

"And what did you say?"

"Not much, I suppose."

I glared at her.

"Not *much*? Whose life *is* this they're talking about?"

"Mine. Trouble is," she said, "I know what they mean."

"Eh?"

"They're right. Even you say the same thing. I *am* bliddy hopeless."

"Hell's teeth, Ella. Don't put *me* on their side."

"And they say I can't come round so much. And this sleepover thing . . ."

"This *sleepover thing*?"

"It's getting out of hand."

"Out of hand?"

"They say it's what little girls do. They say it's fine when you're in junior school. But this is not appropriate."

"What?"

"They say an occasional Saturday might be OK, but . . ."

"And what did *you* say to all this?"

"Not much."

"Not *much*? Bliddy *hell*, Ella."

"And that Easter thing . . ."

"That *Easter* thing?"

"Yes. That is right off the cards."

"What?"

That Easter thing. It was the thing we'd all been planning since the depths of last winter when the sleet was splashing down and we thought we'd all get beriberi or something for the lack of sun. The *North*! We wailed. Why do we live in the frozen *North*? Why not Italy? Or Greece? We laughed. One frosty night we sat outside The Cluny with our breath swirling around us, all tucked in tight together to keep the heat of our bodies in. Sod this, we said. We'll make our own Italy! We'll make our own damn Greece! Where? In Northumberland, of course. We'll go first chance we get, in the Easter holidays, in spring. There should be at least a bit of sun by then. If there's not, we'll just pretend there is. We'll get drunk and dream there is. We'll go to the beach for a whole damn week. We'll get the bus, or we'll hitchhike there. We'll take tents and sleeping bags and camp in the dunes. We'll take guitars and flutes and tambourines and drums. We'll take a couple of massive pans, a ton of pasta, gallons of pesto, a thousand tins of tomatoes. We'll take a binbag full of frozen bread. We'll save up and stock up on boxes of Lidl Chianti and Aldi Chardonnay. And up there we'll catch fish from the sea. We'll nick spuds from farmers' fields. We'll light bonfires and have beach parties every night. We'll sing and dance and get away from Holy bliddy Trinity and from Krakabliddytoa and from *Paradise* damn *Lost*. We'll forget about anticipated grades and adjusted grades and passes and fails and averages and stars and all the stupid boring bliddy stuff that stops us being *us*.

Yes! It was going to be great. It was going to be the kind of thing we thought that being sixteen and seventeen would bliddy *mean*. We were going to be free!

And now here's this. Here's the boringest farts in the whole damn world stopping my best friend from sharing it with me.

"But, *Ella*," I said.

"I know," she answered. "But, Claire, it's different for me, isn't it?"

"The adoption thing, you mean?"

"Yes. The adoption thing. Without them, I'd be . . ."

"What?"

"Nothing. You know that, Claire. Absolutely nothing."

FOUR

We went anyway, the rest of us, just like we said, first chance we got. We broke up for Easter on the Friday, started heading north next morning. I couldn't travel with Ella, so I chose to go alone. I wanted to experience that thing of being just me, moving on my own across the earth. An adventure, even if it lasted just fifty miles or so. I told the others I'd hitch but I found I didn't have the nerve. I took a tangled route to make sure I crossed nobody's path: a string of local buses zigzagging north from town to town, coastal village to coastal village. My rucksack was heavy with tomatoes and wine. Beyond Alnmouth the bus passed Carlo and Angeline flat on their backs in the sunshine in a field. At Boulmer I saw a rapidly running figure I took to be Luke. I'd told myself I'd start to write a journal and I scribbled empty comments on the beauty of the spring, the flashing of the sea, the darkness of cormorants on a dark wet rock.

I wish Ella was here, I wrote, and I wrote it at least twice again.

In the bus shelter at Beadnell, I tried to write some poetry.

Come on, I whispered to myself. *Something, come!*

No good. I abandoned it.

Too early, I told myself. *Mebbe in a day or so.*

We gathered at Bamburgh, as we'd planned, on the field below the castle. All of us were there by three o'clock. Each of us was welcomed with whoops and hugs. We moved onto the beach and followed it a mile or so southwards, to where the beach was wide and the dunes were high and where the view of the Farne Islands, scattered eastward across the sea, was most intense. We gathered driftwood as we walked. The sky was clear. The sun burned golden as it fell towards the Cheviots.

We pitched our tents in the dunes and laid our sleeping bags inside them and made our first fire on the beach. We ate pasta and drank wine. We sang. We yelled and whispered at the beauty of the night, the stars, the moon, the turning of the lighthouse light far out on Longstone, the shushing of the sea, an owl's persistent call from somewhere not too far behind. And shooting stars, a little storm of them for ten minutes or so at two a.m.

We stood at the edge of the sea and held hands and swayed and sang.

"My bonny lies over the ocean . . ."

"We all live in a yellow submarine . . ."

"Bobby Shaftoe's gone to sea . . ."

As we tired, we changed, and our voices and our bodies became stiller, more driven, and we chanted chorus after rising chorus of "The Magpie" into the deepening night.

"Devil, devil, we defy thee

Devil, devil, we defy thee

Devil, devil, we defy thee."

Later, in my tiny tent, I texted Ella.

Oh you should be here.

She phoned immediately back.

"Tell me," she whispered.

"It's just lovely," I said. "What are you doing?"

She laughed.

"Deciding how to please them so I can come with you next time."

"Good!"

Before I slept, I heard the lovers among us making love, and a guitar, and someone singing as clumsily as I'd been writing poems.

FIVE

I hardly slept. We swam next morning, when the sun was hardly risen over the Farnes. I threw my clothes off as I ran to the water, and others did as well. The sea was cold as ice, but we had a blazing fire to run back to. We pulled on our clothes, wrapped ourselves in blankets, wore scarves and hats and ate huge bacon rolls and drank from tin mugs filled with steaming tea. Right from the start there was always someone singing: low breathy choruses of shared voices, outbursts of wild wailing, leaps into ancient Border Ballads and old Tyneside tunes. The tide was out, and we searched the rock pools as we had as children. I plucked a crab from its hiding-place beneath a stone, held its shell between my fingers while its legs and claws waved in the empty air. I put a fingertip between its claws and grinned at the tiny nips it tried to give. The heads of hooting seals popped up from the sea.

"Hello!" we called. "Hello, seals! Hoot hoot hello!"

They dived out of sight, surfaced again in a different place, looked at us again, hooted again.

"They're answering us!" we called. "Hello! Hoot hoot! Hello! Hello!"

Terns danced above the shallows and gannets plummeted into the depths.

Michael stood on tiptoe and pointed far out and yelled,

"Dolphins! Look! Bliddy dolphins! There! And there!"

We looked and said we couldn't see, then said we thought we saw, or were they just the patterns of the waves? We kept on looking, looking.

"Yes!" I said. "There, look! There!"

Then Michael said they'd gone, and maybe they'd never been there at all.

A few families roamed the beach now. Children splashed in the shallows and dogs leapt in the surf as the tide turned and the sea came in again.

We went to find more fuel for the fire.

It was Angeline who discovered the snakes in the dunes. She didn't scream, didn't run. I was close by. She crouched, called me softly.

"Claire! Claire!"

She held up her hand, beckoned me towards her,

finger pressed to her lips, eyes wide with astonishment and warning.

There were two of them, curled up on a pathway through the marram grass, just two yards or so away from us.

I held my breath. The sun poured down on them. Motionless, they gleamed, rusty-brown, dark zigzag patterns on their backs.

"Adders," breathed Angelina.

"Like you could just reach out and touch them," I said.

I leaned forward, arm outstretched. She caught my arm.

"They'll bite," said Angeline.

Now Carlo was with us.

"But wouldn't kill," he said.

"No?" I said.

"Not venomous enough. Enough to kill a dog, a sheep, but not one of us. Not you."

"Oh, look!" gasped Angeline.

One of the adders started to uncurl. We saw its forked tongue flick. Carlo stamped the sand and the other uncurled. One slithered across the other, then both of them slithered away from sight, into the grass.

We gazed at the strange tracks left in the sand. I leaned down and traced them with my fingers.

"There'll be dozens of them," said Carlo. "All coming out for spring."

"So beautiful," we whispered.

Beautiful. Such a privilege, to see such gorgeous things that spent so much of their existence in darkness, in the earth, unseen.

"Wish I'd dared to touch," I sighed.

There was hectic drumming from the beach, the sound of waves crashing onto the sand.

"Anybody else feel famished?" I said.

We hurried back down. We ate hot beans from our tin mugs, swiping them up with chunks of sliced white bread. There was hardly any water, no one wanted to walk to the village to find some, so we drank beer and wine. Michael came from the dunes with an armful of fence posts. He threw them down beside the fire for the night.

I wish you were here, I texted to Ella.

Me too, she texted back.

It's beautiful & wild. The sun shines down.

It's dull. I'm at my books. It's cold.

There are seals and crabs. We think we saw dolphins!

Dolphins! Oh I wish that I could see!

Imagine them!

Dark arcs leaping through the waves.

And we saw snakes, Ella!

Snakes?! Keep clear. You must come back home safe again.
They're harmless. Are you being good for them?
A paragon. They say they're very pleased with me.
xxxxxxxxx
xxxxxxxxx

I tried to write poetry again. I leaned back against the sand and wrote that the islands seemed to float, that maybe the whole world was a floating thing, that thoughts were like dolphins that leapt out from our depths to surprise us, that dreams were like snakes.

"Leap like dolphins, poems," I whispered. "Crawl out of me like snakes."

Sam Hinds came to sit beside me. He had a bottle of red wine in his hand. He asked if he could read and I shut the notebook and said no.

"I'm squiffy," he said. "I've always meant to tell you this. I think you're great."

I laughed out loud and swigged his wine.

"I mean it," he said. "You're strange and beautiful."

"Sing me a song, then."

"What?"

"That's what songs are for, to celebrate strange beauty, and to entrance the one you think is beautiful."

He laughed and started on a made-up song.

"O Claire you are lovely

O Claire you're so sweet
O Claire lalalalalaa
You're good enough to eat."

I told him that was worth a kiss and so we put our arms around each other and kissed.

I pulled back.

"Don't *really* eat me, Sam!" I said.

Then I jumped up and ran to the jetsam that lay in the space between the wet sand and the dry sand. There were great dried-out stalks of kelp, lengths of rope, bits of fishing net, shells, dead crabs, plastic bottles, pebbles, chunks of smoothed glass and smoothed brick. I started pulling fragments out, laying them on the sand where it curved up into the dunes. I made the outline of a body. And of course others came to help me make it beautiful. We made a long figure with sticks for limbs, pebbles and stones for flesh, trails of seaweed laced with crab shells, sea shells and limpets for his hair.

"Woman or man?" said Angeline.

Michael put a stretch of bulbous kelp for a penis and we cheered and laughed.

We dropped bright green seaweed on him for pubic hair. We gave him two round pebbles for his balls.

We gave him one green eye and one blue, and made his pupils from seacoal. He lay gazing into the afternoon sky. We sat around him and sang and drank. Some of us swam again and this time the water seemed even colder, but I stayed in long enough to float hand in hand with Sam Hinds for a while. The swell lifted us and let us fall, lifted us and let us fall. He sang his song for me in time with the swell through chattering teeth.

Back at the fire we danced to warm ourselves. We thumped rocks together as drums. We whirled dry seaweed through the air. We played guitars, whistles, tambourines. We put strands of grass between our thumbs and blew to make screeching sounds. We cupped our hands and blew into them to sound like owls. We screamed like the gulls above and we hooted like the seals. The sea splashed and rolled and the sand and pebbles seethed. We held hands and we danced around the fire and the man. We laughed to see families with their children and their dogs slowing, stopping, heading back to where they'd come from.

"We are wild things!" we yelled. "But we will not harm you!"

The sun shone down.

"Thank you, sun!" we yelled. "Oh, you're so damn hot!"

"This is not the North!" we yelled. "This sea is the Mediterranean. This land is Italy! This land is Greece!"

We played and danced through the afternoon and into the gathering dusk.

Then became still again, which seemed so right when the earth became so beautiful. Rose-red sky above the dunes, the fire smoke rising in gentle clouds, birds heading homeward over rocks and sea, a single dark ship far out with its brilliant light. Darkening sea blending with darkening sky. The islands darkening, the light of Longstone beginning to flash and turn. A sickle moon, thin as a fingernail paring. The first stars. The deepening dark and the constellations beginning to be visible. We all knew the simplest ones—the Great Bear and the Small Bear—and we named them quickly. Carlo traced and named the others for us.

"Orion," he said. "The Hunter. Corona Borealis, Northern Crown. And oh, the Great Dog. See it there and there and there."

"You could see bliddy anything, couldn't you?" I said.

"Yes. And the stars that look connected are really nothing to do with each other, except on our minds, in the old stories. There's the Swan. See? Cygnus, flying through the heavens as it has for a billion years!"

We stared into the universe and tried to turn the stars into these shapes. We said yes we could and no we couldn't.

"And The Harp, look. Lyra. Its bright star is called Vega. The strings lead down to Sulafat and Sheliak. You see?"

Angeline played the strings of her guitar.

"No," she said. "But I can hear it. Hear?"

"Yes," we said.

We sat in silence and gazed up in wonder, as if the constellation really was giving its music to us. The flames leapt and the embers glowed. Our faces shone and when we met each others' eyes we widened them and could say nothing. It was like we were one single thing, all of us together making one being.

I thought of my friend in her narrow home.

Ella, you should be here.

I let Sam Hinds put his arm around me but I thought of her.

Ella, you should be here.

We drank our beer and wine.

When night gathered all around us, when the dark was truly dark and the stars were truly bright, we sang and danced again, and we did these things wildly. We yelled our youth and our freedom and our joy and they rose with the flames into the Northern night.

We sang again, as we had last night.

"Devil, devil, we defy thee!
Devil, devil, we defy thee . . ."

We sang boldly, bravely, then softly and more softly.

Sam came with me into my tent that night. Even then I thought of her.

Ella, you should be here.

When he slept, I texted her.

You should be here. It's very beautiful. We made a man. We danced beneath the stars.

It's three a.m. I think I'm asleep.

Sleep on. Dream of me here. Dream of when you'll be here too.

xxxxxxx

xxxxxxx

SIX

It was soon after dawn when I heard the music close by the tent. I looked at my watch: 6:00 a.m. Too early. Another almost-sleepless night. My head was sore, my mouth was dry. I pulled the sleeping bag over my head, closed my eyes, searched for sleep. Sam shifted and snored beside me. The music went on.

"Stop it," I wanted to yell. "It's far too bliddy early."

Then a voice was singing with the strings, breathy and lovely, halfway between a woman's and a man's.

Not a tune I knew, not words I knew, not a voice I knew.

I nudged Sam, whispered his name. He stirred, didn't wake.

There was no sound from the sea, no breeze against the tent.

I shuffled from my sleeping bag, pulled some clothes

on, crawled to the door. The sea's horizon burned, and the air above it shimmered, ready for the sun to show itself. I crawled out. I shuddered. There were the marks of a snake in the sand just outside the door. I stood up and saw him. He sat on the slope of sand just above the jetsam man. He didn't turn to look at me. Just went on playing, singing, face turned towards the sea.

"Hi," I said.

No answer.

He went on singing, playing. I slithered down the dune to him. Others were coming. Carlo, Angeline, Michael, Maria.

"Hell's teeth," breathed Maria at my side.

"Who's *that*?" said Michael.

"And what the hell is that *song*?"

We didn't go close. It was like we were all scared. We just stood there, crouched there, knelt there, listening. He wore the shabby purple coat, the ancient blue Doc Martens, the thin red scarf. That long black hair, held back with ribbon or string. The down of dark beard on his face. Dark blue eyes, edged jet-black. Hard to tell how old he was. Like us, maybe a bit older than us.

He glanced at us, that was all. He played on, and the song sweetened, intensified.

The sun rose and his face turned golden in its light. The song sweetened, intensified.

The others came out of their tents, came down from the dunes to the beach. His song sweetened, intensified.

We cursed in amazement at what we were hearing.

"Oh, Christ," breathed Maria. "Oh, *listen*."

Then all we could do was gasp and sigh.

Like something from dreams, like something from the soul's depths, like something from somewhere none of us believed in, none of us had ever been.

It felt clumsy and wrong, but I fumbled in my pocket for my phone. I rang her number.

"Just listen," I whispered.

I held the phone out towards him.

"Oh, God," I gasped, as I saw the birds coming down from the sky to the beach, as I saw the seals lift their heads from the sea, as I saw from the corner of my eyes the adders slithering down the sand to us.

"Ella," I breathed. "Even the *snakes* are listening."

SEVEN

He wouldn't look at anyone, not properly. Eyes shifted away just before they met another's. He put the guitar down after a while. Guitar? Not really. It was a clumsy-looking, homemade-looking kind of thing. A block of wood, the neck, the strings, some keys for tightening. Seemed made of driftwood, waste wood, any wood. But when he played, it sang so sweet, so deep. Even the clunks of the thickest strings were right. They held the music down to earth even as it seemed to float away to nothingness. The crudeness and the sweetness rang together, like the body and the soul, the earth and sky. And his voice. Like something from a billion miles away and somewhere very close. Like something ancient, something very new. How can I say this? Wouldn't have known to say such things just a few short months ago.

Anyway, he put the instrument down on the sand beside him.

I held the phone to my ear but the battery had gone. Ella had gone.

"I heard the noise ye made," he said.

His voice was like ours, a Northern voice, but he licked his lips each time he spoke as if they weren't used to having spoken words on them.

"Heard ye in the night," he said. "So I came."

"Who are you?" said Angeline.

His face clouded, as if the question troubled him. He didn't answer.

The birds that had gathered flew away. The seals dipped out of sight. I looked back and saw nothing but the marks of slithers on the sand.

He reached down and touched the jetsam man.

"That's good," he said.

"Would you like something to eat?" said Carlo. "None of us have eaten yet."

"Aye."

He watched Carlo reviving the fire, then opening a pack of bacon.

"Not that," he said. He pointed. "Some bread. And that as well."

"Apple."

"Aye."

"Banana?"

"Aye."

He stared at us like we were ghosts, like he wasn't certain he was seeing us at all.

"Who are ye?" he said.

We told him our names.

"Where did you come from?" I said.

He turned around, towards the dunes, and the distant Cheviots beyond the dunes.

"Over there," he said.

We named some towns: Alnwick, Rothbury, Wooler, Ford.

"No," he said. "I wander. I play music and wander. Where's this?"

"Bamburgh Beach," I said.

He bit into the bread. He looked towards the sea, the islands.

"Oh aye," he said. "I remember it."

"Will you play again?" said Angeline.

"Yeah."

"Will you teach me how to play?"

He shrugged.

"Why not?"

He picked up the instrument again and plucked the strings, played some delicious notes.

He looked at it, as if he himself was amazed by it.

"Me name's Orpheus," he said. "Aye. It's Orpheus."

And he played and sang again.

EIGHT

Maybe we were mad that day. Maybe some of the things that seemed to happen didn't really happen at all. Maybe many of the things that seemed to happen in the days and weeks that followed didn't really happen. Maybe it was all because we were young, and because being young is like being mad. Maybe just being human, at any age, is a bit like being mad.

But maybe the best things that we do, and the best things that we are, come from madness.

He played and sang and the beasts came back. The birds and the seals, the snakes in the dunes. And this time when Michael gasped, "Dolphins!" we really did see dolphins, and we saw them come back again, and back again. We saw them close to shore, the beautiful arcs of them breaking the surface and curving through air. The tide came in and as it came it seemed so calm. No crashing of waves onto the beach, just a gentle turning of the water as it rose, as if the sea itself had ears and had come to listen. And when the pebbles and sand seethed with the water's coming, they seethed in time with Orpheus' song.

Ballocks? Maybe. Who knows? Maybe it's all distorted by memory, but I know what we saw that day. I know what we felt. It was like being blessed. Like truly becoming ourselves. Like being loved.

I saw the burning of desire in Angeline and Maria as they gazed at him. I saw James entranced, already falling, falling. I saw the wakening of new desires in Michael and Sam.

We sang with Orpheus, but our voices were just a pulse beneath his weird lovely melodies. Angelina played along with him. We tapped our sticks and rocks and drums to give percussion. We swayed our bodies. We danced on as the water rose towards us. And we forgot ourselves. We were not there. We weren't these people with these names on this beach. We were lost in the music. We were gone.

We spent the whole morning like that.

When Orpheus stopped, he shook his head and laughed, like he was as amazed as we were. He held the instrument before his eyes.

"Hell's teeth!" he said.

"What is that?" said Angelina.

"This?" he said. He shrugged. "It's a lyre."

His brow furrowed as he gazed at it.

"Aye, that's it," he said. "It's my lyre."

Angelina had moved so that she was right at his side.

She reached out and touched its strings. They clunked.

"Did you make it yourself?" she said.

"Wouldn't know how. It was give to us, ages back."

He handed it to her.

"What do I do?" she asked.

He shrugged.

"Just sort of pluck it," he said.

She tried again.

Clunk. Clunk. Clunk.

"Use that," he said, pointing to her guitar.

"But it's nothing," she said.

"Neither's this."

He laughed at a seal that had come right out of the water and was now flopping its way back towards it again.

"Daft thing," he said.

And he hooted like a seal, properly like a seal. The seal hooted back and flopped on into the sea.

"Don't try too hard," he said to Angeline as she started the guitar. "You know how to do it so just do it."

She strummed a few notes.

"Go on," he said. "Just let it play."

He leaned over her, touched her hands.

"Gentler," he said. "That's better. Aye. Hear it?"

Yes. It was better, better than we'd heard her play before.

"That's right," he said. "It's just like breathing. You're off now."

He ignored, or didn't even notice, the eyes she gave him as she played. He didn't see Carlo's stare. He didn't hear Maria sighing. He laughed at the disappearing seal.

"I forgot all this," he said as if to himself. "But it's been here all the time."

He stood up and went to the water's edge, took his boots off, waded, ankle-deep, spread his arms wide as if at the joy of it.

Michael opened some white wine, passed it round and we swigged it down. It tasted sour, salty. Maria said she was desperate for water, but we knew that nobody wanted to find some, not right now. We swigged the wine and passed it on. Angeline continued playing. Her playing grew sweeter, more intense. She stared towards Orpheus as if she was playing just for him.

"Cut it out!" said Carlo suddenly.

"What?" she said

"That! You're just copying him."

"I'm not. It's nothing like him. It *couldn't* be anything like him."

"Oh no. *Course* it couldn't."

He spat into the sand.

"What the hell's wrong with you all?" he said.

Orpheus came back, his feet all sand.

"I'll be off, then," he said.

"What?" I said. "Where to?"

He shrugged.

"Just wandering," he said. "Here and there and somewhere else."

"You can't just . . ." said Angeline.

"Can't just what?" he said.

He sat down and dusted the sand off and pulled on his boots again. He looked at their soles and smiled.

"These've done a fair few miles," he said.

He picked up his instrument.

"Play for us again," said Maria.

"Eh?"

"Just a bit. We've never heard anything like it, Orpheus."

"Have ye not?"

"No," I said.

He looked into the distance, to the north towards the castle, across the sea to the islands, to the south along the broad white beach, to the west beyond the dunes to the Cheviots.

"I dunno," he said. "I wanna . . ."

But he sighed again and relented. He plucked the strings, and his impatience left him. The sea grew still. We grew still. He sang, he sang, he sang and if there was a way to put music into words I'd do it. If there was a way to fill the spaces between words with the sound of him, the sound of the sea, the sound of the birds, the sound of the breeze in the grass of the dunes, the sound of the rolling pebbles and the turning sand, I'd do it. He played, and it felt as if we were filled with life as we listened, and as if we almost died. Somehow I managed to think of Ella and I took out my phone. Somehow there was some power in it again. I dialled her number and held the phone out so that she could hear him.

"Just listen," I whispered before she could speak.

He played and sang. He saw the phone and laughed.

"Who's that?" he said.

"My friend," I managed to say.

"Why's she not here?"

"They wouldn't let her."

"*They!*"

He came closer. He took the phone from me and grinned and put it to his lips.

"You should be here and all," he said. "Tek no notice of *they*."

Then he sang directly into it, soft, sweet, hypnotic.

I thought of her, in her boring narrow house with her boring narrow parents, lifted away from all that boring narrowness by Orpheus' sound.

"Who are ye?" he said.

He repeated it.

"Who *are* ye?"

He sang again, with eyes closed, held the phone to his lips as if he wanted to pour himself with the sound right into it, and into Ella's ear. Ella, the beautiful dreamy one. I imagined her now, with the phone to her cheek, dreamier than ever, lost in the music just like we were, gone.

I imagined her silence.

Orpheus laughed.

"Speak to us!" he said. "Tell us your name."

I imagined her dreamy whispery voice as she struggled to reply.

"Ella Grey," he said. "Now speak again, Ella Grey."

He listened. He laughed softly.

"This is a song for Ella Grey," he said.

And he breathed a low sweet song into the phone and into Ella's ear so many miles away.

Then silence. His face seemed to darken.

"Say yer name again," he whispered.

"Aye," he sighed. "Just like that, Ella."

He sighed as she spoke. He sang a few more lingering notes to her.

Then he placed the phone into my hand.

"She's called Ella Grey," he whispered.

"Yes. Ella Grey."

"She must be very beautiful."

"She is."

He closed his eyes.

"I see her," he breathed. "Hell's teeth, I see her there."

Then he slung the lyre across his back, turned away from us, headed into the dunes.

"Orpheus!" Maria called. "Don't go yet!"

He turned back for a moment and held up his hand against the brightness of the sky.

"Don't follow," he said. "I'll find ye. You'll find me."

"How?" I said.

"Because we have to."

Then he was gone. We did try to follow after a time. We went to the top of the dunes. We saw his footsteps, the slither marks of snakes. We saw his black hair in the distance, his purple coat appearing and disappearing. Then we weren't certain if we saw. There, we said, as we had with the dolphins. And there! Then it was over, and the dunes and the fields beyond were just the dunes and the fields beyond. The silence was just the breeze and the sea.

Orpheus had wandered. He was gone.

I whispered into the phone.

"Ella."

But the phone was dead.

Ella was gone.

NINE

That afternoon clouds gathered out at sea. Beautifully illuminated drifts of rain fell on the Farnes. The sea became more turbulent. Luke and Lorraine took empty wine bottles to Bamburgh village for water. They filled them at taps outside the public toilets on the main street. A policeman saw them.

"Who are *you?*" he snapped. "What you doin' *here?*"

He didn't let them answer.

"Are you the ones been making mayhem on the beach?"

He took a notebook out. He wrote down their names.

"You're not eighteen, are you?" he said. "What you doin' drinkin wine? Who d'ye think ye are?"

He confiscated the bottles.

"The fun's over. We don't want the likes of you up

here. Decent folk didn't want their peace disturbed by half-crazed townies. You understand?" he said.

They nodded.

"We want you gone. I'll be there with the dogs tomorrow. I expect to see no sign of you."

They came back with a couple of bottles of lemonade that we shared. We kept the fire burning and we ate some beans and bread.

Angeline played her guitar.

"It's weird," she said. "How can I get so much better in such a tiny amount of time?"

Carlo glared at her.

"It's called practice," he said. "You've not stopped playing the bliddy thing since we got here."

She turned her back on him.

"What'll we do?" said Michael. "Can they really send us packing?"

"We're not harming anybody, are we?" said Maria.

"Let's stand our ground," said Angeline.

Carlo snorted.

"Stand your ground. Who do you think you are? Che bliddy Guevara?"

We drank wine and beer. We did some dancing and stamping. We found ourselves yelling the name of Orpheus, maybe just celebrating what he'd brought to us, maybe trying to somehow call him back.

"Why did he go like that?" said Angeline.

Carlo spat.

"He's a chancer. He's trying to mystify us."

"No," said James. "He's more than that."

Carlo grinned.

"Oh aye?" he said. "So it's not just the girls that he's got gagging."

James blushed and cursed and looked away.

"D'you think he *will* find us again?" said Angeline.

"He found us today," said Maria. "He said he heard us, so he came."

"Orpheus!" we yelled. We hooted like the seals and screamed like the gulls, and we laughed at how daft it seemed. But there was passion in our laughter. We wanted him again, his voice, his presence.

"Orpheus!" we yelled into the darkening air and into the yearning inside ourselves. "Orpheus!"

As night came we gazed at the constellations, which now were being crossed by scudding clouds. We looked for the Dog, the Swan and the Lyre, as if they could help bring him to us. We couldn't see them right, but Carlo wouldn't help us. We yelled our words towards the sickle moon. The light of Longstone lighthouse swept across us and swept across us, moving us from shadow to light, shadow to light. Soon, drizzle fizzed on the embers.

I slept with Sam again that night. Rain pattered on the tent as we made love. He seemed so clumsy. His muscles, honed by years of going to the gym, seemed too solid, too manly. I lay awake and listened to the rain and wished more than ever that Ella was here. I wanted to talk to her, to sleep with her. I started to become strangely troubled by the thought of her. What if something's happened? I thought. What if when I get back she's no longer there? I told myself not to be stupid. But what if? I asked myself. What if she's gone?

I kept hearing the song that Orpheus had sung to her. So beautiful. But what were those deeper notes I now heard in it, the grief that was in it?

By dawn, I was trembling with fright at the thought of her.

I was already packing by the time Sam woke.

He grunted something.

"I'm going back," I said.

"Now?"

"Yes."

"Why?"

"I just want to."

"But this is great!"

"Is it?"

"What about your tent?"

"It's wet. And you're still in it. You can have it. You can bring it back if you like. Or just leave it."

"Claire!" he said as I left but I didn't turn back.

There was cloud from horizon to horizon. The sea was grey, the islands black. The ashes of the fire were wet and black. I walked over the jetsam man. I hurried along the beach, by the jetsam line. There was a dead seal washed up among it. There was the droning of a foghorn somewhere and the lighthouse light still flashed, paused, flashed again. I ran beneath the castle walls into the village. A bus was groaning to a halt outside The Star. I jumped on board.

"Single," I said.

"Where to?"

"Where you going?"

"Ashington."

It was in the right direction.

"That'll do."

The driver rolled his eyes.

We travelled south, through Seahouses with its amusement arcades and its chip shops and its lobster pots and fishing boats; past the jagged ruins of Dunstanburgh Castle jutting into the sky; past the airfield at Boulmer, its security fence, its cameras, its warning signs. We turned inland and moved across the ancient

Northumbrian coalfield, past its abandoned mines, its turved pitheaps, its blocked-up shafts. Behind me an old man wheezed, and coughed into a handkerchief. A little child sang *The wheels on the bus go round and round, round and round, round and round.* All so ordinary, so commonplace, but inside me everything so turbulent, filled with weird joy and dread. Rain splashed on the windows. I saw it gathering in pools in the fields, running down into roadside gutters. I took out my notebook and tried to write and found my hand seeming to move of its own accord. Words moved beyond the weird dread, beyond the coughing of the old man, beyond the rain and the grey sky, and as they moved they said how beautiful this all was, all this stuff I passed, every little bliddy insignificant thing, the fall of a raindrop across the pane, the tiny crack in the seal of the window, the patterns in the skin on the back of my hand, the squeak of the bus as it turned, the bowing down of the trees before the breeze and rain, the gathering of water into rivulets and streams, my beating heart, these flowing words—how all of this, each fragment of each fragment, was extraordinary and must be praised.

The world, I wrote, *and everything in it, is all an amazing song. What we have to do is bliddy sing it.*

I laughed out loud as the child sang louder and sweeter.

I turned round and applauded him. His mother flinched: who was this, this weird scruffy writing lass, turning on the bus to her lovely bairn? But maybe she saw the joy in me, because she relaxed, and smiled, and clapped the baby's hand and said,

Look, this lady thinks you're a grand singer.

In a bus shelter just outside Ashington, with the rain falling in sheets before me, I wrote again. Nothing that really made much sense: just names of things, and invented words and imaginary words and words that swooped across the pages like birds and flowed over them like water.

There was a colliery museum nearby. I glanced towards it and the wheel over the shaft started to spin. This is how it would have spun years ago to drop pitmen and pitboys down into the depths. I shuddered at the thought. I shuddered to think of the earth all pockmarked with holes, of the tunnels deep down beneath me now, of the tunnels spreading everywhere inside this earth. I looked at the ground beneath my feet and it seemed just an illusion. At any moment it could collapse, crack open, and down I'd fall through potholes, sinkholes into spaces that hadn't been entered since a distant age. I stopped writing at the thought of such darkness and danger, of the deaths that had occurred in the world below. And my anxieties about Ella came flooding back, and I shuddered and trembled again, and turned my eyes from the wheel and forced myself to write again. To write her name as if I was calling her, as if I was singing her. *Ella, Ella, Ella!* To write the beauty of the world around me. To make words sing to keep Ella and the world alive. And the words helped lift me out of the darkness and dread and back to that light.

And then a bus clattered to a halt in front of me and I clambered on and it carried me back towards the Tyne.

TEN

I went straight to her place, the square grey house on the slopes above the Tyne. Her mother let me in.

I knew that nothing had gone wrong, nothing apart from the usual sense of wrong that always shadowed Mrs. Grey.

"You're back quick," she said through thin pursed lips.

"Yes."

She made me aware of my shabbiness, the dirt on my skin, sand in my hair, scent of firesmoke, stale-wine breath.

"So it would have been a waste, wouldn't it, for her to go? Too much for you, was it?"

I put on a smile.

"It was wonderful, Mrs. Grey."

"Was it now? She's upstairs studying should you need to see her."

"Thank you."

"Don't stay. She is in mid-essay. And you appear to need a shower and some sleep."

Ella hugged me as I went into her room.

"Was she horrible to you?" she said.

"No."

"What brought you back so fast?"

I shrugged.

"It rained."

It sounded pathetic.

"What about turning Northumberland into Greece?" she said. "What about bringing Tuscany to the North?"

I shrugged again. Why *had* I come? Why didn't I turn around and go straight back now? It would be easy.

"I missed you," I said, again pathetically.

She smiled and hugged me.

"Me too," she said.

I picked up her essay.

Discuss the Connection between Earthly and Divine Love in the Holy Sonnets of John Donne.

I dropped it again. Yuk. That was something I'd have to answer in a week or so.

"I was worried about you," I muttered.

"*Worried?* About *me?*"

"Aye."

"How silly!"

"I thought something terrible had happened, or was going to happen, or . . ."

"And here I am, all fine, just the same as ever. Ella Boring Grey."

She laughed.

"You!" she said. "Too much imagination, that's you."

I sighed. *Me*. Me and my daft anxieties. I sat on the bed. I looked at the photograph of her on the wall. She's two years old in a bright white dress and it's Adoption Day. Mr. and Mrs. Grey, both dressed in grey, lean down to hold her hands as if they want to hold her forever and forever. Another: first day at school. She's in a red checked dress with her hair in ringlets and a little rucksack on her back. And me and her, tied together for a three-legged race on school sports day. Ordinary stuff. The kind of photographs we have at home of me. And a shelf of books and posters on the wall and a dozen types of makeup and the iPod and the CD player and a mug of pens and dirty coffee cups and clothes scattered on the floor and this little house with Tyneside all around and the river flowing nearby. Ordinary. Ordinary.

Mrs. Grey called up the stairs.

"Ella! Don't forget there is work to complete today!"

"She wants me gone," I said.

"Listen," said Ella. "She says if I really knuckle down, it should be possible for me to come next time."

"That's great."

"Yes. So be extra nice to her. That'll help as well."

"I'll try."

She looked at me then burst out giggling.

"Well?" she said. "Are we not going to talk about it?"

"About?"

"About the *wonderful* thing that happened when you were gone."

"The wonderful thing?"

"Stop playing *games,* Claire. Him, of course!"

"Orpheus?"

"Duh! Orpheus."

"But it was just a few minutes. A few seconds. A . . ."

"Yes! But you said yourself how incredible it was."

"Yes," I sighed.

She took my hands in hers.

"It was something I'd never heard before, and something I'd known all my life. It was like something I'd known *forever.*"

She squeezed my hands tight.

"You must have all felt it, too. You did, didn't you?"

I looked away.

"Yes. We did."

"To hold the phone, to listen, to imagine you there with him, to imagine him there with you, and to hear that song."

"So what *did* you imagine of him?"

"Ohhh." She grinned and did her dreamy look. "Golden hair, slender limbs, pale loose clothes, clear blue eyes . . ."

"He's nothing like that."

"Ah well. Never was one for the imagination, was I?"

"Claire!" called Mrs. Grey. "I really think it's time now!"

"Is he there still, with the others?" said Ella.

"He went away."

"But he'll come back, won't he?"

"He said he would."

"He'll come and find me."

"Will he?"

"Of course. He has to. Mebbe next time we're at the beach. Mebbe earlier. He couldn't sing to me like that and never sing to me again. Go on. Go home. Toe the line now, and we'll get wild later."

She led me to the front door.

"Sleep deep," she whispered. "Dream of him."

Kiss.

Grin.

"Just think," she said, "if you hadn't phoned, I wouldn't have heard a bliddy thing."

"No," I said.

Thud, went my heart, then *thud* again.

"That's true," I said.

Kiss. Kiss. *Thud.*

ELEVEN

Carlo was the only one who came back that week. I saw him one afternoon in the street, and waved, but he turned away. All of the others stayed. Then they appeared in ones and twos, in dribs and drabs.

We gathered on our bank of grass outside The Cluny.

"Why did you leave?" they asked me. It was just a squall. The sun came back, bright as ever. The sea calmed down, everything dried. And yes, the policeman came with his dogs, but he was so much kinder now. He said that mebbe we should just move further down the beach, away from where the families went. He said he didn't want to be a killjoy. Been young himself one day, believe it or not. And could tell us a thing or two himself about nights on Bamburgh beach. Nudge nudge, wink wink. Michael caught fish on a line. We cooked them on stones at the edge of the fire. The pasta and tomatoes lasted for days. We spent an evening in the Victoria bar and got paid in drinks for singing songs to Angeline's melodious guitar. Carlo? Aye, he'd had enough. Said we were all a bunch of daft bairns. Said Angeline was more in love with her damn guitar than she was with him. He told us to grow up, and he shoved off all alone. A bunch of kids from Gateshead arrived. They were just like us, mental and bright. They brought fresh supplies of wine. They had a flute and a tin whistle and two guitars. The music we all made! We partied deep into every night. Orpheus? No, didn't come back. Not another sight of him. But sometimes it was like he was there with us. We told the Gateshead kids about him. We said if you listened really hard, you'd hear him singing somewhere, so we all just shut up and start listening and pretty soon we're whispering. Yes! Bliddy yes! There. And there and there! And even the kids from Gateshead hear him, even though they've never even seen him nor heard him in the first damn place. Aye, we've got drink inside us, and aye, we're fired up simply by being there, but we hear him, Claire, his singing in the night. Orpheus. How can that be? Oh God, it was magic. Oh God, you should have *stayed*. It was so great. It was everything we bliddy wanted. We were so *free*. And you weren't *there* . . .

And even now, with the others beside The Cluny, it

was like I wasn't there. I still had that weird dread. I wanted to be with Ella, only Ella. But she loved being with the others, not having to try too hard with anybody or anything, being lovely dreamy Ella, singing along, dreaming along. It was like *she* wasn't there, not really, like she wasn't *anything,* like she was just an empty space, waiting to be filled by something, by anything.

And it's like I was nothing, too, like I was waiting, too. But mebbe that's just how it is when you're young. You've got all these weird forces in you, but you feel unsatisfied, empty, unfinished. You feel like everything that matters is a million miles and a million years away, and yes it might come to you but no it bliddy mightn't. It'll be like an unreachable constellation of stars. And nothing will happen, ever. And you'll never be anything, ever.

I wanted to stop myself thinking at all. I wanted to sing with the others without thinking about being myself singing with the others. I wanted to sing like sweet Ella did.

I kept up my thing with Sam. We slept a couple of nights together at his house. It didn't really mean much. His parents didn't seem to mind much. I wanted to love like him.

Push push push push! Come come! Lovely! Sleep.

But how can you turn yourself into something you want to be when you're already what you *are*?

I tried to work, to write my essays. I tried to lose myself in thinking and writing about Donne and Milton. But my thoughts and words kept slipping, slithering, sliding back to thoughts of Ella, of Orpheus and Ella. They were already tangled together in my mind.

"Is everything all right?" Mum asked one day.

The holidays were almost over. School loomed on the horizon. The undone work was heaped up in my bedroom.

"Aye," I said

"All OK with your mates?"

"Aye."

"And Sam."

I shrugged, nodded.

"Aye."

She smiled. I think she knew how it was with him.

"Then why all this moping about?"

"Dunno."

"Dunno! God, how youth is wasted on the young!"

She cuddled me.

"You, madam," she said, "take things far too seriously. You're *young*. *Be* young. You'll never have it back again, you know. Go out! Be free!"

"I've got to work," I said.

"Work?"

"Those essays, Mum."

"Essays! They work you far too hard. If I had my way there'd be no school from spring to autumn. What kind of essays?"

"Love."

"What?"

"I've got to write about love."

She flung her hands up in despair. She burst out laughing.

"Hell's teeth, that says it all! What's the point of getting the young to *write* about love? They should be *doing* love!"

TWELVE

Ella helped. Yes, she was a dreamer, but she had a way of doing her work without any fuss. She didn't understand the struggles that some of us went through. If you had to write 1,500 words you wrote 1,500 words. You put one word then another then another then another. You said the things that Krakatoa said you were supposed to say. You didn't think too much, and didn't expect too much. You handed the work in on time. You ended up with a B or a C or a very occasional A, and no matter what Krakatoa or your parents said, that was more than good enough. You certainly didn't waste your precious energy yearning for A stars. It was easy. So why the fuss? Why the stress?

She finished her work well in time. Then she came to my room to help me. She sat on my bed while I sat at my little desk.

"Just *do* it, Claire," she said. "Nobody else is going to, so just do it."

She filed her fingernails. She hummed a few tunes.

"By the way, the Greys are now firmly wrapped around my finger," she said.

"Really?"

"Really. I showed them four essays, all neatly printed out. They were all stapled, with title pages and word lengths, each neatly tucked up in its own transparent plastic wallet. That's the kind of thing that really impresses them. *The Earthly and the Divine: An Essay by Ella Grey. 1,523 words.* They just love it! I read them a bit where I blather on about the music of the spheres and Plato's Theory of Forms. Remember? That stuff on Krakatoa's handouts? Anyway, it bliddy bowled them over. 'Oh, Ella, that's so lovely! How on earth do you know such things? See? You can do anything when you set your mind to it. Oh, we are so proud of you!'"

I told her I was proud of her as well.

"Ha!" Then they went on to the reminiscing, which always helps me to get what I want. They told the tale like they always tell it, as if I've never heard it all before. The baby in the basket on the hospital steps in the deep midwinter. How they became excited straight away. How they rushed to the adoption office. All the interviews, all the agonizing, all the praying, all the hoping, all the forms. But it was all for the best because look at this beautiful bright young woman, and look at these two happy parents! They got the photos out: me in the basket, me in their arms with the nurses and doctors all around. And the cutting from the *Chronicle:* "Who Could Abandon Such a Lovely Thing?"

"It's true," I said. "Who *could* abandon a thing like you?"

She shrugged.

"Anyway," she said. "Looks like I'll be at the beach next time, and looks like I'll be able to kip at yours again."

"Really?"

"Really. See the benefits of getting essays done? So get them bliddy done."

I stared at my blank page.

"D'you think you'll ever find out?" I said.

"Eh?"

"Who it was that left you there? Why they left you there?"

"Not now," she said. "But I guess I'll always find myself looking at the people on the street, thinking that could be her. Or it could be that couple there. But I know they could be anywhere. They could be dead. And then sometimes I forget it all, and just think the Greys are my proper parents."

"That's mebbe for the best."

"Aye, it is. And I do love them, even though I moan about them."

I wrote my title: "The Earthly and the Divine." I groaned. I stared into space.

"I've been having these dreams," she said softly.

"What kind of dreams?"

"Dunno. Dunno if they're mad."

"All dreams are mad. Tell me."

"Been having them these last few weeks. I hear voices, the voices of my parents, singing me to sleep."

"Your real parents?"

"Yes. I don't see them, but somehow I know it's them. And I feel them holding me, like they never want to let me go."

"Are the dreams nice, or . . ."

"They're lovely. And they get all mixed up with the Orpheus dreams. I hear him singing as they hold me, like he's coming closer, like he's trying to find me . . . And I call out his name to bring him to me . . ."

"*Weird.*"

"Aye, weird. *I'm* weird!"

She drew her nail file over the cuticle of her thumbnail.

"Ha!" she said. "Mebbe the Greys are right. They got themselves a fairy child."

THIRTEEN

Sunday night before school started again, we went down to The Cluny. Everyone but Carlo was there. He'd given up on us. All of us were glum.

"The gates are slammin' shut!" we sang.

"The shutters are clankin' doon!"

"The prison house awaits us aal!"

"And Krakatoa!"

"Aaaagh!"

"Bianca!"

"No!"

"Crystal Carr!"

"Aaagh! No!"

We giggled and drank cheap wine.

"Been great, though, hasn't it?"

"Aye!"

"And we'll go back again."

"Yeah!"

"At half term!"

"Yes!"

"So not too long to wait."

"And this time you'll be staying, Claire!"

"I will."

"And Ella will be there."

"Oh yes, she will be there."

"And Orpheus will return!"

"Oh yes," whispered Ella at my side. "He will return. I will be there."

We broke up early, headed home early. Homework to check, schoolbags to pack, sleep to be got. I walked with Ella. When we were alone, she took my hand and turned me back again, following the path alongside the Ouseburn.

Couldn't see in the falling dark if she was smiling.

"What we doing?" I asked.

"Just follow me. Want you to do something with me. Won't take long."

We came to where the water flowed through its locked gateway from below the city. The place was darkened by the banks around it, by overhanging trees.

"Take your shoes off," she told me. "Roll your jeans up. Go on. Just for me."

I laughed and did as she asked.

"Now be still."

Below us the water caught the lights of the stars, of the city's glow in the sky, of the lights in the windows of The Cluny. It glittered and swirled.

"That water's come from everywhere," she said.

"Eh?"

She put her finger to my lips.

"Hush, Claire."

Now her face was close to mine. She closed her eyes.

"Water," she whispered.

She spoke as if the words were flowing out of her, as if she just spoke them as they came to her, as if she was in a dream, and I held my cheek to hers so I could feel her close and feel the vibration of the words as they ran through her and ran through her.

"This water's come from everywhere. From in the hills, the Cheviots, the Simonsides, the Pennines, from little springs high on the moors, from spouts in the rocks and streams in the fields and it flows downhill and gathers strength and mixes and accumulates, and flows and flows, across the land and under the city and under our streets and homes and it flows out here through its gates and it keeps on flowing and it'll flow down The Tyne to mingle with the sea and it'll be lifted again and it'll fall again as rain and flow again across the land and under the city and under cities all across the world and it'll flow out through these gates and through all the gates like these . . ."

She paused. She smiled. She moved her face away from mine.

"We learned it in primary school. Remember? In Miss Bates' class. The Water Cycle. Sea to sky and sky to earth and earth to sea and sea to sky and on and on and on it goes and when it will stop nobody knows. I thought I understood. But now I really do."

She put her finger to my lips again.

"Now listen to it, Claire. Yes. Listen to how it gushes and trickles and flows. But listen as well to the music it makes as it comes through the gates. Can you hear them vibrating?"

I listened. I couldn't.

"Are you OK?" I whispered.

She smiled.

"Yes. Just a wee bit cracked."

She stepped onto the steel ladder that led down a concrete slope to the water. Then she stood in the water and her face bloomed in the dark as she looked up at me.

"Come on, Claire," she said.

I stepped down and stood beside her. The water

wasn't even knee-deep. There was that sour sickly smell to it. All kinds of rubble and litter on its bed. She waded through it towards the gates. I followed, moving my bare feet tentatively. Tried not to think of the litter and filth and trash that were often trapped in the bars of the gate. Tried not to think of rats and fiends and monsters. She took my hand and drew me to her, then she touched my fingers to the bars.

"Feel it?" she whispered.

Yes. I felt how the bars vibrated with the endless flowing of the water over them.

"And hear the music they make?"

Did I? I felt and listened. Yes, a humming, a faint droning that mingled with the sound of the water's flow. I felt and heard the chinking and rattling of the chains and bolts and padlocks. I heard the tip tap of the warning sign.

She came close against me again.

"The gate is like his lyre, Claire," she said.

"*What?*"

"Yes. And like your phone."

"My *phone*?"

"When I heard him on the phone, it was like I heard everything, Claire. That there was something coming through him and through the lyre and through the phone and into *me*. And now it's coming with the water through the gate. Listen to it. *It* is *him*."

"What is?"

"Everything. The water and the music it makes. The music of everything. It is *him*, and we were with him for a little time."

"Oh, Ella!"

She heard the concern in me.

"It's all right," she said. "I'm not going crazy. And, Claire, it ties up with my dreams."

"Your dreams."

"Of before the Greys. I'm all alone in a dark damp place with music in it. I hear their voices, his so deep and hers so sweet. I feel them holding me and never wanting to let me go. I hear music flowing like water."

"But, Ella, that could be anybody's dream of how anybody started. It's just the bliddy *womb*!"

"It's different. Orpheus makes the dream clear. The music in the dream is *him*. The music in *everything* is him. Look at *us*, Claire."

"What do you mean, Look at us?"

"Look how we're standing in the water. Listen how it flows across our legs. Listen to the sound it makes as it flows across us. Can you hear?"

"Yes, but it's just what happens when . . ."

"It's *him,* Claire. Be still, and listen. *We* are his lyre. He plays his music and sings his songs upon *us.*"

"Oh, Ella."

"I'm not mad. I feel like I'm just starting to wake up."

"Oh, Ella."

"I've known him before, Claire. And he's known me. He's known all of us. You have to believe it."

I could say nothing. We stood there in the water, at the place we used to run screaming from because of childhood nightmares, and now we stood there like it would bring some kind of bliddy grace.

Her eyes shone bright, reflecting the rising moon.

"Oh, Claire," she gasped. "He's on his way. I know it. He's nearly here."

FOURTEEN

And he came on a Thursday morning, in the middle of Krakatoa's lesson, a couple of weeks into the new term. There he stood, in the shimmering at the edge of the schoolyard, and she went out to him and walked away with him, and the tale of the two of them, the tale of all of us, suddenly leapt forward, and we had to hurry to keep up.

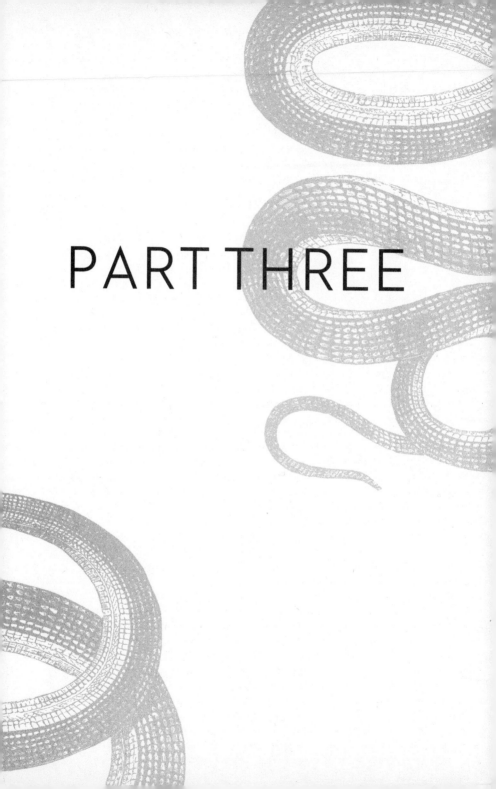

PART THREE

ONE

"He wants to marry me, Claire."

"What?"

"He says in all his travelling, he's never met anybody else like me."

"And who the hell have *you* met?"

"Nobody. But he says the same as me—that he's known me always."

"And you're only *seventeen!*"

She giggled. She shrugged.

"I *know,* Claire. It's crazy."

"Then what . . ."

"But it makes a weird kind of sense."

"Sense?"

"It's like he understands me, like nobody ever has before."

"Hell's teeth, Ella!"

"He does! And I feel like I exist more than I ever have before."

"But it's . . ."

"It's *what?*"

"It's infatuation! It's just because he's charmed you."

"It's not. It's impossible to explain, but I *feel* it, Claire. I *feel* it."

We were in my room. She'd been with him all that day, ever since jumping out of Krakatoa's lesson. She said they'd been just wandering here and there. Just talking, just dreaming. They'd walked right down by the river to where it flowed into the sea at Tynemouth and they walked all the way back again. Sometimes they'd stopped and he'd played the lyre and he'd sung.

"And you were right," she said. "The birds flew down. Fish were jumping in the river. A couple of dogs followed us everywhere we went. It was like they all loved him, Claire. All the beasts, all the birds. Once I looked at the river and thought that even that was changing its course to flow towards him. It was like being in a dream but the dream was real."

"Jesus Christ, Ella. It *is* a dream."

"But you said the same things yourself. You said you saw them happening."

I took her by the shoulders. I wanted to grab her by the throat.

"But *marriage,* Ella." I laughed out loud. "And it's hardly as if the Greys are going to say, 'Oh yes, Ella, that sounds absolutely bliddy fine to us.'"

"It's all right. They won't need to know."

"What?"

"It won't be one of those boring stuffy *wedding* things."

I sighed. I waited.

"He said we don't need all the trappings—priests and churches and registrars and all that stuff. It'll be a true coming-together of bodies and souls, like it was in the past, before everything got caged by rules and regulations."

She kissed me.

"It'll be lovely, Claire. We're going to do it on Bamburgh Beach. At half-term, when we're all there. Afterwards we'll meet up in secret when we can, then when I've left school we'll be together properly. We'll go wandering together. Ella and Orpheus. Orpheus and Ella."

I groaned.

"Hell's damn teeth, Ella."

"It'll be simple and beautiful. Just music and dancing. Some wine. Some sunshine. And love." She kissed me again. "What better place for it? What better way to turn Northumberland into Greece?"

She giggled.

"Don't be so serious," she said.

She took an apple from my bedside table and crunched into it. She smiled and said she was bliddy famished. They'd been so preoccupied with each other they'd eaten nowt all day.

She laughed at me.

"Oh, Claire, can't you just be happy for me? Yes? No?"

She stood right before me. The light from the window poured in from behind her. Oh, she looked so beautiful. She looked so changed, suddenly more than the dreamy Tyneside girl. She looked as if she was shining.

"Be happy. Please. At least for today. Yes?"

I shook my head.

"Yes," I told her. "At least for today."

"Good. Now I have to go. And listen, the Greys mustn't suspect anything. You won't tell them anything, will you? You won't tell them I left school today. You won't tell them about Orpheus. You won't tell them about me marrying him at half-term."

I sighed at her ridiculous list.

"No," I said. "I won't tell them."

"Good. And, Claire, I want you to give me away."

"Give you *away*?"

"It's what the father usually does, of course, but I don't have a proper father, so I want it to be you. I want you to put my hand in his and give your blessing. Please say you'll do that."

I couldn't say a word.

She gripped my hand. There was sudden distress in her lovely eyes.

"You've been everything to me," she whispered. "Ever since the day we met at primary school. Remember?"

"Yes, of course I remember."

Miss Simpson's class, all those years back. Two little girls at a little wooden desk singing together, counting together, chanting the alphabet, the days of the week, the months of the year. Two little girls holding each other's hand beneath the desk and whispering that they were each other's very best friend and would always be so, and were always so as the years passed by.

"Then say you'll do it for me, Claire. *Please.*"

I looked at my poor delighted distressed friend. What could I do for her? How could I prevent this all happening? There were a few short weeks between now and half-term. Maybe it all would change. Maybe she'd see sense. Maybe Orpheus would disappear. Maybe . . .

"Say it, Claire."

I tried to please and comfort her, as I always had.

"Yes," I said. "If it comes to it, I suppose I will."

"Brilliant!"

She giggled again.

"Oh, it'll be such fun!"

She turned to go.

"Oh, and I want him to meet your parents," she said.

Jesus Christ.

"I can't take him to meet mine, can I?" she said. "Your parents will understand him. They know about people like him. And I've always felt so close to them. Please say I can bring him. Please say yes."

TWO

They came that Sunday evening. I didn't tell Mum and Dad much in advance, just that he was a lad we'd all met at Bamburgh, that he was a singer, that he'd come to see us all again and had met Ella.

Mum laughed.

"Is it love?" she said.

"Who knows?"

"Ah well, let's hope so, at least for a little while. She really deserves a nice boy." She winked. "As do you, madam."

Then she cuddled me and told me Sam was fine and to take no notice of her.

I said that Ella would like them not to speak to the Greys about him.

"So they don't know about him?" said Mum.

"No. So best if you don't tell them. Not yet anyway."

Part of me wanted them to snap back, "Yes, we will tell them, and right now!"

But Mum just said, "They are rather overprotective, aren't they."

"Rather?" said Dad. "Anyway, when do our paths ever cross theirs?"

"So he's a bit challenging for them?" said Mum.

I shrugged.

"I suppose so."

"Well, it's great she feels she can bring him here," said Mum.

"Quite an honour, in fact," said Dad.

"What does he eat?" asked Mum.

"Vegetarian, I think."

"Ah. Excellent!"

Ella had said they'd come at four. It was almost six by the time they turned up.

"I'm so sorry," said Ella. "We lost track of time. If it's too late . . ."

"No," said Mum. She took Ella's hand and drew her in. "And this must be Orpheus."

"Aye," he said.

She stepped aside and guided them into the kitchen.

"You're very welcome," she said. "Call me Elaine."

I was waiting with Dad at the kitchen table. Ella was

wearing a long blue flowery flowing thing and strappy sandals. He was like always: the coat, the boots, the lyre, the hair.

"I'm Tom," said Dad.

"Claire," I said. "Remember?"

He cast his eyes over me. He blinked.

"I was on Bamburgh Beach," I said.

"Oh. Yes."

So weird, to see him in a kitchen, in a house. On the beach he'd seemed at home, but here he was uncertain, awkward, edgy.

Mum took his coat from him. He had blue jeans and a worn blue shirt beneath. He rested the lyre against the table leg.

"What will you drink?" said Mum.

"Wine?" said Dad. "You girls could have some as well."

Orpheus turned to Ella. She squeezed his hand.

"Juice," said Ella, "if that's OK. Or just water."

"Water," said Orpheus.

We all sat down. There were platitudes: about Ella's work at school, about her lovely dress, and whether her parents were well.

"So you sing, Orpheus?" said Dad.

"Yes."

His gaze roamed across the walls, the Picasso print, the African masks, the shelves of pasta and beans and chilli sauces, the dangling garlic, the Le Creuset pots.

"And are you from around here?" said Mum.

"Kind of."

Close to, I saw how beautiful he was. Cheekbones, jaw line, full lips, clear dark blue eyes, skin unblemished beneath the scrawny beard. And I saw how beautiful Ella had become, as if he'd reached deep down towards the beauty that had been in her always and had drawn it out into the light and enabled it to shine.

"He likes wandering," said Ella. She squeezed his hand again. "Don't you, Orpheus?"

"Aye."

Ella laughed.

"I think he's been everywhere," she said. "Far more places than I've ever been!"

His eyes kept moving, as if he was just waiting to be gone again. I watched Ella watching him. She'd go anywhere with him, would follow him anywhere.

"We're travellers as well," said Dad. "Or have been."

He reached for the lyre.

"Do you mind?" he asked.

Orpheus shrugged.

"No," he said.

"We saw things like this in Kashmir," Dad said.

"And Marrakech," said Mum. "All those musicians in that marketplace!"

"The Djemaa el Fna," said Dad. "Otherwise known as the Square of the Dead. And those conjurors and snake charmers! Wow."

Orpheus nodded.

"You've been to such places?" said Mum.

"Yes."

"So marvellous, aren't they?"

Dad plucked a couple of the strings. The notes sounded dead, flat. He laughed.

"I never had the musical touch," he said. "You'll play a bit for us."

"Tom," sighed Mum. "Leave the lad alone. He hardly knows us yet."

There was a plate of falafel, another of dolmades, a bowl of salad, lots of bread, water, juice. Ella said how delicious it was, how she never got food like this at home. She talked about her walk with Orpheus that morning. They'd followed the Tyne westward. They'd seen salmon jumping, canoeists on the river. There was a whole blossoming hawthorn tree spinning in the current that must have been washed out from the banks further upstream.

"And those daft ducks!" she laughed. "Remember, Orpheus."

He narrowed his eyes, remembering, and he smiled at her.

"Yes," he murmured. "Daft ducks. Oh, aye!"

The quack of a duck came from his lips and we laughed.

"Thought we'd never get rid of them," said Ella. "They'd have followed us to the end of time!"

He ate some lettuce, a couple of dolmades, a tomato or two. He sipped his water.

"We went to the Ouseburn," said Ella. "And I told him about when we were little." She laughed. "That's why we were late. We took a little detour into the past."

"They were such lovely little girls," said Mum. "I see them now, with their dolls and their summer dresses and . . ."

"Mum . . ." I said.

"I know. And where were you a little boy, Orpheus?"

"A little boy?" he said in surprise.

"Yes, when you were a bonny little boy? Were you somewhere around here?"

He seemed confused, like the questions were difficult for him.

"Yes," he said. "Not too far away."

He looked at Ella nervously. Yes, he wanted to be away.

"And your parents. Can I ask . . . ?"

He rolled his eyes upward.

"In Heaven," he said.

"Oh. I'm so sorry."

"That's all right."

We had some fruit afterwards. Orpheus accepted some hibiscus tea. The day outside darkened. Ella said she'd have to be gone soon. She said that everything had been lovely. She said thank you for accepting Orpheus into your home.

"Perhaps . . ." said Mum. She indicated the lyre. "If he wouldn't mind, before you both go . . ."

Ella smiled. Orpheus shrugged. All the awkwardness fell from him. He lifted the lyre, started to pluck its strings, to make the deep notes and the high notes, the warm and the cold, the dark and the light, to draw these things together in the music. He started to hum, then to make separate sounds, some of them like words, some of them like birdsong, some of them like the cries of beasts, the laughter of children, the whispers of lovers, their groans of joy. And we leaned towards him as he sang and played, we began to lose ourselves in him, we disappeared, we felt that the music he played came out of us. I don't know how much time passed. Time was nothing. Time was gone.

And when it was done, he simply stopped singing, stopped plucking his lyre. We came out of our dreamless dreams and he was already putting his coat back on, he was already taking Ella's hand and helping her from her chair, and they were both leaving us and opening the door alone and going out into the dark.

We watched them go. We sat together, mother, father, daughter, at the kitchen table. Nothing we could say. The wind chimes were chiming upstairs. Birds were singing, birds that should have been silent at night. The house itself seemed to tremble, to vibrate. And the table, and the chairs we sat on did also. And our hearts, and ours souls, had a music in them that must have been always there but that until now we had not heard, had not known. But now we did, for Orpheus had been with us, if only for a little time.

THREE

I heard him play once more before he went away again. Outside The Cluny, of course, where we and others like us gathered, where we lay at fretful ease on the sloping grass to dream of being artists, where we explored the ways of love and friendship, where we trembled with the weird joys and pains of being young and getting older, where we yearned for freedom and ached just to belong. And as he played, they came out from the workshops and the bars, they hurried down from the bridges, they came running from the pubs and restaurants on Newcastle's quayside. And they all slowed as they came closer, as the sound possessed them. Some tried to hum along but soon were silent. Impossible to keep up with him. Impossible to imitate. There must have been two hundred or more gathered around the boy in the dark coat with the lyre in his hands, with the Ouseburn flowing through its gates at his back. He sang, and played, and enchanted, and many fell in love with him that night, but the only one he looked upon was Ella, my friend Ella Grey.

And then he was gone, as was his way, and she went with him for a little while.

And we who were left behind came to our senses.

Who the hell? What was that? How did he do that?

And then Bianca and Crystal were at my shoulder, with Carlo between them.

Crystal licked her lips and clung to Carlo.

"I tell you," Bianca whispered. "If I don't have that Orpheus before I die . . ."

FOUR

How could someone change so much? How could she suddenly know so much, think so much? Krakatoa was astonished.

"Ella Grey, you amaze me. How has what I have been saying for months suddenly got through to you?"

"I don't know, sir," she told him.

"I have not changed my methods. I have not been aware of you giving me greater attention. Have you been reading widely?"

"No, sir."

"Perhaps your parents have been helping you a great deal."

"They always want me to do well, sir."

"Of course they do. And your father is . . ."

"A joiner, sir. And Mum's a cook."

"Indeed. Truly the ways of the mind are mysterious."

He strolled through the aisle between the desks.

"Tell us again your thoughts about Mr. Milton and his *Paradise Lost* if you would."

"Sir?"

"About the apple, and destiny, and free will."

"Well, sir. God knows from the very start how things will turn out. He knows that Adam and Eve will be thrown out of the garden. He knows that trouble after trouble will be the result."

"Did Adam and Eve not have the chance to make things turn out better? What of free will? They didn't *have* to eat the apple, did they?"

"They did, sir. They had a kind of free will, but it wasn't *really* free will. If it really was, it would be in conflict with God's knowledge, and in the world of *Paradise Lost,* that could not be allowed."

"So they *had* to do what they did?"

"Yes, sir. God put the apple there. He made man and woman. He made their nature. Because of that, he knew what they must do, and they chose what they were destined to choose."

All of us were watching her again in astonishment. Was this the Ella we knew?

"So their apparent free will?" said Krakatoa.

"Was part of their destiny, sir."

Krakatoa laughed.

"What a conundrum Mr. Milton sets us, Miss Grey!"

"Yes, sir. He does."

He put his hands on his hips. He regarded her from on high.

"Do you believe such things yourself, Miss Grey? That our lives are shaped by forces beyond ourselves?"

"No, sir. I believe in freedom, sir. Milton wrote at the time of Milton. That time is gone."

He smiled at her. He shook his head.

"Miss Grey, you have sat in silence and dream for these past months and now you begin to come out with this. Is this what you have been daydreaming of all this time?"

"I don't know, sir. I wasn't aware of daydreaming of anything in particular, sir. I was just kind of . . ."

"Empty?"

"Yes, sir. As you often told me yourself. Empty."

He laughed again.

"Maybe it's just Milton, sir," she said.

"Milton?"

"Maybe that's why he's a great poet. He gets through to you even if you don't believe what he believed, and even if you're a bit thick. And maybe poets get to you best when you're sort of dreaming, when you're hardly there at all."

Krakatoa groaned, from deep within.

"Oh, perhaps, perhaps. But goodness gracious, what does that say about teaching methods? What does that say about analysis, about writing essays, about . . . But best not to think of such things, perhaps."

He scanned us all.

"Miss Finch?" he called.

"Yes, sir?" said Bianca.

She paused in her nail-filing.

"Have you any light to cast on the obscure ways of the poetic voice?"

"Dunno about that, sir. But Ella certainly looks different, sir."

"Does she now?"

"Yes, sir. If you ask me, looks like she's been getting a proper good seeing-to, sir . . ."

Krakatoa rolled his eyes.

"Ye Gods!" he muttered.

He turned back to Ella.

"You have illuminated us on John Milton, Miss Grey. You have shone light onto the metaphor of John Donne. What other gifts are you about to bring us as time goes by?"

She smiled.

"I don't know, sir."

"Ha. Perhaps more daydreaming is in order."

"Yes, sir. Perhaps it is."

He watched her for a long time.

"*What* is it?" he asked her.

"I don't know, sir . . . I don't know what you *mean,* sir."

"Nor do I, Ella Grey. Nor do I."

FIVE

"Are you?" I asked her as we walked home that day.

"Am I what?"

"What Bianca said." I tried to make a joke of it, tried to imitate Bianca's voice. "Are ye gettin' a propa good seeing-to, pet?"

"I've hardly seen him yet."

"But . . ."

"But we find places." She smiled. "We've made love, if that's the word for it."

We walked on.

"And?" I said after a time.

"And . . ." She looked away from me, towards the river, towards the earth. "And it's like it's nothing to do with me, and not even anything to do with him. It's like we disappear, or something."

"Oh."

"Yes."

We walked on.

"Is that what it's like with Sam?" she said.

"You're joking."

We giggled softly together. Lovely Sam. Mr. Muscle. We came closer to our homes.

"It's like I'm not there," she said. "But it's like everything is in me. It's like I can't explain . . ." She suddenly crouched down and touched a daisy growing by the concrete path. "It's like I'm this daisy and it's like the thing that's in the daisy is the same as the thing that's in me. The thing that pushes it up from the earth and pushes the petals out and makes the pollen glow. It's like the thing that pushes the song out from those birds and makes them spread their wings and makes the salmon swim and . . . Oh, Claire, how the hell do I know?"

I laughed, and crouched beside her.

"It's like a feeling," she said, "and it's like a sound, and it's like being me but being nobody and being everything but being absolutely nowt at all!"

She took my hand and touched my fingers to the daisy.

"It's like being in love with this bliddy daisy, Claire. It's like being in love with the bliddy river and with the bliddy sky. How crazy is that?"

"Maybe it's wonderful," I murmured. "It's maybe what first love is really supposed to be like."

"Is it? I don't know. I've only been with him for a little time but I know we'll be together always and we've always been together always."

I took a breath. I took her arm and guided her to her feet.

I took another breath.

"Ella," I started. "I wonder if you should . . ."

She pressed her fingers to my lips.

"No, Claire," she said. "Don't say that."

"Don't say what?"

"Anything that stops it, Claire. Anything that makes me doubt."

SIX

How did the weeks pass by? In the way that all time passes by. In seconds that turned to minutes that turned to hours that turned to days that turned to weeks. Time passed by in routine, in work, in drudgery. In descending into sleep by night and rising to the light by day. In waking, washing, dressing, eating, drinking, brushing hair and cleaning shoes, in checking school bags, in walking along the riverbank on schooldays with a single friend and entering the stream of others to pour yet again through the metal gates of Holy Trinity. In being on time, in being prepared, in walking in an orderly manner through the corridors. In being cheerful and cooperative and polite. In attending to the teachers. In listening to Krakatoa snap and inform and speculate and bore and occasionally illuminate and grumble and groan. In reading Milton, Herrick, Donne. In making notes and writing essays and doing hour after hour after hour of homework. In showing that we were diligent students who wished to do well. In showing that we were modern young adults who understood their world, who knew what was expected of them, who were realistic but ambitious, whose future prospects were deeply important to them. In showing our parents that we were all they could have wished for, that we wished to achieve all that they wished us to achieve. We were fine young people. We were civilized and industrious. We should be rewarded with a time of play. We deserved to be allowed to go together at half-term for a break on Bamburgh Beach.

I was extra nice to the Greys. I shook my head in astonishment with my parents at the wonders Orpheus had performed in our kitchen that night. I agreed with them that yes, it was marvellous that I was beginning to come upon such interesting people in my life. Yes, I told them, maybe I'd meet him again when we travelled north to Bamburgh. Yes, I'd pass on their greetings. Yes, I'd be sure to invite him to visit us again. I'd tell him he was always welcome at our door.

And I gathered with my friends on the grass beside The Cluny. And we whispered our excitements, as always, and we broke into music and song, as always, and we yearned to grow much older and to be forever young, as always always always.

And when I woke alone in the dead of many nights, I tried to calm my fears, and to still the thuds of weird dread. I tried to tell myself that this was all just a playful thing, a kind of game, a teenage fantasy. Why shouldn't Ella have a mock-wedding? Why shouldn't she, and all of us, have a day of daft joy?

And I found ways to tell myself that it was all just stupid, anyway. Orpheus himself was the fantasy. Ella said he'd gone off wandering again, and that he'd meet up with us again on Bamburgh Beach.

I laughed at this inside.

It's all ballocks, I whispered to myself. *He won't turn up. He's duped us, charmed us, tricked us. He's just a traveller, a singing tramp. He's gone forevermore. Thank God for that. Good riddance to him. Go to Hell, Orpheus. And leave my lovely friend alone.*

I went with her to Attica Vintage Clothes in town. We spent an age going through the rails. She found a pale green silk dress with the label torn out that could have been Biba. I bought a black dinner jacket with a shining satin collar from about fifty years ago, and a pure white smock to go beneath. I bought black shoes with ribbony straps that curled up around my calves. She said she'd go bare-footed. I bought a black mesh hat whose veil angled down across my eyes. She said that I looked stunning and that her own head would be bare, except for those tender pink flowers that flourished in the dunes.

Angeline wrote wedding music to play on her guitar. Michael and Maria bought bottles of Tesco fizz. They found some bottles of retsina in Fenwick's. Angeline made a chocolate wedding cake. We stocked up on cheap wine and beer. We all made cards. Sam found an old copy of *Paradise Lost* and ripped its pages into confetti.

James took to lining his eyes in black, to wearing mascara, to shrugging at our smiles, and blushing as he looked down and whispered, *I know, I know.*

I bought a new notebook in the cheap stationery shop in Grainger Market, a lovely thing with red Italian marbling on the cover. I tried to write poems in celebration of my friend, tried to stop my words from swerving into gloom. I found myself stealing lines and images from Donne. I must not weep. I would not lose my friend. She may go off for a time from me, but she'd return, as when a pair of compasses is closed and the points meet up again. We would be forever joined, whatever happened with her Orpheus.

Remember me, Ella, I wrote. *I am the one who is true.*

On the first Saturday of half-term, we took the X18 from Haymarket Bus Station.

We sat at the back, all the friends, all the hipster crew.

I sat with Ella. We held each other's hands, as we had ever since Miss Simpson's class. We passed the black war memorial with the angel bowing down towards the desperate soldiers. We passed the university, where many of us thought we might end up. We drove past the town moor with the herd of unmoving cattle on it. We watched the houses of the city, the offices, the shops, the swimming pool, the library. Traffic and walkers headed back to where we'd come from.

We moved out from the city on the Great North Road towards the empty spaces of Northumberland.

Ella squeezed my hand. I leaned close to her.

"Farewell, my ordinary world," she said.

SEVEN

We sang songs from childhood as we headed further north.

My bonny lies over the ocean.

Nobody seemed to mind. We sang sweetly, good-humouredly. We were nice young folk, no bother to anybody. Some little boys sitting with their mothers sang along with us.

The day was fine, sun shining on the fields, breeze making the tips of the trees dance. We left Tyneside behind, we crossed the ancient healed coalfield, we saw the sea shining. At Amble, bright boats danced their way to Coquet Island. Beyond here, the road followed the coast, and the beautiful places started, the places of dunes and castles and long white beaches. Sparkling rivers danced to the surging sea. There were stone-built harbours, and little natural harbours called havens. Fishing boats rested on shingle and lobster pots were stacked up by black timber sheds. Orange nets were stretched out across the rocks to dry.

We whooped and pointed through the windows as we went through Seahouses.

"Oh, I used to love this place!" called Michael.

"Fish and chips from Coxons!"

"Those boats from the gift shop made out of shells!"

"Yeah! And rocks shaped like walking sticks and full English breakfasts!"

"And sugar dummies!"

"And mermaids made of sea coal!"

"And that ice-cream shop there!"

"And look! The kipper man!"

We twisted in our seats as we drove on, to look back and remember until we could see no more.

And then the miles of dunes right by the road, and the Farnes stretching away across the sea, and then the great red castle on its rock above Bamburgh village, and the thrill of arrival, the thrill of hauling out rucksacks and bags from the bus, and walking in a happy crew down The Wynding to the beach, and the sound of the sea, and the scent of it, and gulls screaming above.

EIGHT

We went to the place we'd been before. We put our little tents up in the dunes. We made our fire. We went plodging in the sea and searching in the pools. We drank wine and we sang. No sign of Orpheus that first day. I was so pleased that we were still free. Time passed and I danced with Ella arm-in-arm and cheek-to-cheek beneath the gathering stars. Our feet shuffled through the delightful sand. The Longstone lighthouse light swept across her, showing her and obscuring her, showing her and obscuring her.

"You're so beautiful, Ella," I told her.

I tried to tell her more, but the words I had were not enough and the sounds came out as useless gasps and murmurs. I just held her close, closer. I ached to protect her from all darkness, all pain, and all death.

She shifted away when I asked if she'd like to sleep in my tent tonight.

"No," she told me. "Think it's best if I'm alone. Have this sense that if I whisper his name, if I make myself dream of him, then he'll know exactly where I am and where to come."

She kissed me. I sighed, and maybe she heard the trouble in my sighs. She hesitated a moment.

"I don't think you understand yet," she said.

"Understand what?"

"How much I love him, Claire. And how much he loves me."

"But . . ."

"We would do anything for each other."

"But . . ."

"Maybe you can't. Maybe nobody can unless they've known it for themselves."

"But . . ."

"It's stronger than anything, Claire. It's what keeps the sea flowing, what keeps the stars shining, what keeps us all alive."

Sparks rose from the fire and shooting stars fell down.

"One day you will," she said. "You'll meet your own Orpheus and *thud,* you'll fall. Night night."

"Night night, Ella. Love you, Ella."

"Love you, too."

She carried the glow of the fire on her back as she stepped into the dunes.

I looked up into the night, but without Carlo, none of us could name anything except the simplest constellations, those we'd known since we were bairns.

Sam was sitting by the rock pools. He said he'd seen a fish that seemed to shine.

"Luminous," he said.

I watched with him. Yes, a little flicker then another.

"Do you *get* such things as glow fish?" he said.

"Dunno."

"Me neither. God, sometimes I feel so bliddy thick. Look, there it is again."

"Aye."

"Weird."

I leaned on him.

"Do you want to come to my tent tonight, Sam?" I said.

"Aye. I do."

"Howay, then."

We made love, or what was known as love.

Afterwards I lay awake.

I tried to hear Ella's whisper but the only gentle sound I could hear was the hesitant sea.

I whispered her name.

"Here I am," I whispered. "I'll always be here. You'll always know where to come to find me."

"What?" grunted Sam from his heavy sleep.

"Nothing," I told him. "It's OK."

I stroked his brow. His breathing deepened again.

"Ella," I breathed. "Ella."

I must have slept, because I woke. Still he wasn't there. None of that early-morning singing and playing that I'd heard before. Thank God. So maybe we would get through all of this without him.

Ballocks, it was all just ballocks. Ha!

I crawled across still-sleeping Sam and went outside.

We had bacon sandwiches in massive bread buns. We drank huge mugs of tea. I took some to Ella, but I looked into her tent and she was as still as death. I caught my breath. I lowered my ear to her as my parents told me all parents do when they have their first baby, to make sure the mysterious thing is still alive. She didn't move, she hardly breathed, but yes she was alive.

The boys played war games in the dunes. We girls sat with our feet in the pools and talked about boys. We thought we saw dolphins. There was one great dark thing rolling in the waves that Angeline said must be a porpoise. A couple of seals popped up and down again.

I leaned back and ran my fingers through the sand. I recalled Dad's voice, from years ago, when we sat on a beach like this and he opened my palm and placed a single grain of sand on it.

"Touch it," he said, and I touched.

"Now look at all the grains of sand around us," he said, and I looked.

"There are as many stars in the sky," he said, "as there are grains of sand on all the beaches of the world."

My mind reeled at the idea, as it had done then.

I repeated to the others what he'd said.

"Can that be true?" said Maria. "That can't be true."

"It can be," I laughed. "Count them and you'll find out."

"One, two, six, nine hundred and eighty-three zillion. Yes, it's true!"

"If it's true," said Angeline, "how big is everything?"

We looked together into the empty endless blue.

"If it's true," said James, scattering a handful of sand across the sand. "How small are *we*? And where would *we* be, on this beach?"

No way to know. Time kept on passing by. No sign of Ella, none of Orpheus.

The air warmed as the sun rose higher. We exposed our skin to it. We lay on the sloping sand beneath the dunes. This is what we had wanted, through all that dark winter, through all those weeks of dull routine and working working working.

I swam with Sam. We floated hand-in-hand. We

laughed: this bliddy sea, never any different from bliddy ice.

"Italy!" we laughed. "Greece! What a joke!"

"The North!" I hooted. "It'll always be the frozen bliddy North!"

We swam and ran back to the fire and leaned right over it.

Michael saw them first, at the far end of the beach, coming out of the shadows of the castle. He shaded his eyes with his hand.

"It can't be," he said.

A little group of them, carrying sacks and boxes.

"Can it?" he said.

Hard to make them out at first. There was sea spray around them, sparkling in the sunlight. We didn't want to make them out, didn't want them to be who we thought they were. But they came closer and became clearer.

"It is," said James. "Bliddy Bianca and her lot."

"And Carlo," groaned Angeline.

Bianca started jumping and waving, like she was amazed and overjoyed to see us. She dropped her rucksack in the sand and ran to us like we were long-lost friends.

"It's you!" she said. "Fancy seeing you lot here!"

She laughed.

"This is a turn-up, eh?"

She kept on laughing at our silence, our surly greetings.

"What a shame for you," she said.

She came around the fire to me.

"Diven't worry," she said. "We'll not spoil your fun."

She looked towards the dunes.

"So where's the bride?" she asked.

She scanned the beach, the sea.

"And where's that bliddy gorgeous groom?"

She touched my shoulder.

"Diven't look so fed up, Claire. We heard the whispers. We'll be not a bit of bother. Just ignore us. Pretend we're not here. But, Claire," she whispered. "We couldn't miss this for the bliddy world!"

She turned to the others.

"Crystal! We'll set up camp over there! We don't wanna be in the way of these good folk!"

She ran back to them. They dropped their things thirty yards or so away from us. Carlo unrolled a single big blue tent that they set up awkwardly at the edge of the dunes. They made their own fire, started cooking sausages and beans. They got out bottles of vodka. They set up some speakers and played fast hard music. Pretty soon they were dancing wildly, bumping into each other, grinding against each other, screaming with laughter. They took no notice of us. Bianca took her top off and ran down to the sea with her breasts bouncing. She screamed as she went in thigh-deep, then wildly ran back out again towards their fire.

I went to Ella's tent. Still dead still. Still fast asleep. I went back to the fire and tried to write in my new notebook. Nothing came. I wrote about Bianca and her friends. All of them were half-naked now. Carlo was dancing in flowery shorts. The girls kept hooting with laughter, thrusting themselves at him.

This is a good thing, I wrote. *He won't turn up with this lot here. Be wild, Bianca. Be crazy. Keep Orpheus away.*

Midafternoon there was a burst of sudden screaming from the dunes. Bianca was up there, with Crystal and Carlo.

"Go on!" yelled Crystal. "Do it, Carlo! Yes! Bliddy yes!"

They ran back to the beach, the three of them, grunting with excitement and disgust.

Bianca ran towards us. Two dead adders dangled from her hands. Her eyes were wide with horror.

"I went to pee!" she said. "And these were there! Snakes! Bliddy snakes!"

It seemed like she could hardly breathe.

"Carlo got them!" she said. "Bang bang bliddy wallop with a great big stick!"

Bianca held them up before her eyes.

"Snakes! Aaagh! Bliddy snakes!"

"Aye!" she told Carlo as he came to her. "Aye! I'm all right, mate!"

Carlo mimed the kill again.

"Die, snakes! Die!" he snarled, thumping the beach with his stick.

Bianca whirled the snakes in the air, then wrapped them around her throat and danced in the sand with the terror and the thrill of it.

"Hell's teeth," said James at my side. "This is all we need."

This is what we need, I wrote. *He won't come now.*

Then I looked up from my book, and here he was on the beach, coming towards us, and here was Ella, coming from the dunes.

NINE

Maybe I started to understand it now, as I watched them walk towards each other that afternoon, as they greeted each other, kissed each other, murmured together into each other's ears. They were beautiful, as they'd always been, of course, but their beauty had deepened, sweetened, intensified. They were as much part of each other as the sea was part of the beach, as the air was part of the sky. Terns danced above them as they stood together there, and the edge of the surf sparkled across their feet.

They walked towards us, shining.

"See," said Ella. "He came."

Orpheus smiled.

"Of course," he said to us. "Did ye doubt us?"

He held both of her hands.

"This is my love," he said. "The one I've loved from

the very first moment, the one I loved before I even saw her. And she's the one that has loved me. Who *could* doubt it?"

Ella sighed, and smiled.

"How could I not come seeking her?" said Orpheus.

See, Ella's eyes told me. *Everything is true.*

Bianca and her friends were silent, watching. Then Bianca burst out laughing.

"Bliddy wow!" she yelled.

"That's Bianca and her friends," said Ella. "They go to school with us."

He nodded towards them.

"Bliddy wow!" Bianca yelled again.

"Ding dang bliddy dong!" yelled Crystal.

Carlo stood with his hands on his hips and just stared.

"Do you want to eat something?" Ella asked Orpheus.

He shook his head.

"We'll marry tomorrow," Ella told us.

"In the morning," said Orpheus.

Claire, said Ella's eyes. *Be happy for me.*

So I stood up and hugged her.

"That'll be wonderful," I said. "We'll get everything ready."

I kissed Orpheus on his smooth cool cheek.

"I'm glad you came," I said.

"Really?" he asked me.

"Yes. Yes."

"Good. She wants you to be glad."

Then Orpheus went with Ella to her tent, and we all sat in silence, and gannets flew northwards high above, and oystercatchers pottered across the rocks, and time passed by and time passed by.

And Angeline practised her wedding tune. I uselessly tried to write some kind of wedding ode. James lined his eyes in deepest black. We drank some wine, ate some pasta. The evening was very still. Fine clouds like scattered embers stretched above the Farnes. The birds stopped calling, the hoot of an owl was heard.

Bianca stamped the sand and whirled her snakes.

The sea paused, before the turning of the tide.

TEN

How can I write what happened next? I'm just a girl. A fine young person. Realistic and ambitious. Civilized and industrious. I'm . . .

I spent another almost-sleepless night. Told Sam I didn't want him with me. Listened to the sea and the owls and my steadily beating heart. There was a noise of dogs or foxes coming from the land, and some strange yowling from the sea. Even from here in the shadows of the dunes, through the blue wall of the tent, I saw the turning of the Longstone light.

I listened for Ella, for Orpheus, but there was no sound from them.

Maybe I did sleep, maybe I'm still waiting to wake up. Maybe this is all a . . .

But no. No point in thinking that.

The day began as all days should. The air was still, the

sky was bright. The sun rose golden-red above the sea. I crawled out into the day and saw the sun hanging great and golden above the lovely Farnes. The sea was whispering its way towards us.

Angeline and Maria were already in their wedding-day clothes: mix-ups of jeans and floral dresses. Maria had a necklace of seashells. Angeline wore dolphin earrings and a cardboard tiara she must have made in junior school.

She giggled.

"Glad rags! Not every day one of your mates gets wed, eh?"

We laughed, we lit the fire and made some tea.

Maria had to keep hugging herself with glee.

"Isn't it so exciting!"

The others started coming out. We hauled some stones from the pools and piled them into a kind of rough altar on the dry sand. We put other stones in a circle around it. We put the bottles of fizzy wine and retsina into a rock pool to cool. We opened jars of olives and pickled chillis. We had a box of cheese that was already starting to stink. There were lots of biscuits, some cornflake and rice-crispy cakes, the chocolate cake. We laid out a blanket and rested these things on it.

We kept giggling, gasping, goggling into each other's eyes.

"We're mad," said James. "We must be bliddy mad."

He had dark red lipstick on.

"Get yer togs on, girls!" yelled Bianca.

She stood at the edge of the dunes, breathing great plumes of smoke into the air. She wore a golden metallic breastplate, thigh-length boots.

"It's kicking off?" she called.

"I'll go check on the bride," I said.

I took two mugs of tea to Ella's tent.

"Knock knock," I whispered.

Ella pulled the door aside. There was an intense shining from inside there, as if the light from the risen sun had been concentrated by the orange and white walls of the tent, or as if a new sun shone from within it, from within them. They were naked. Their skin was golden, their eyes were bright. I hardly dared to look at them but I couldn't turn my eyes away.

"Forgive me," I found myself whispering.

Ella laughed.

"Don't be silly," she said. She took the tea. "Good morning, my sweet Claire."

"Good morning, Ella," I whispered. "Good morning, Orpheus."

He whispered, "Good morning, Claire."

I saw how young he was, as young as she, how happy he was, as happy as she. They were teenagers, like me, like all of us. It could have been any of us lying there like them, transformed by love. But *could* it have been any of us? Did it *have* to be these two, Ella and Orpheus, Orpheus and Ella? Were their fates sealed long ago, long before they heard each other, saw each other, long before they even knew the other existed? Was I . . .

I must have been staring, must have been entranced by them.

Ella giggled. She waved her hand before my face.

"Claire. Where are you, Claire?"

I blinked.

"It's *me* that's supposed to be the dreamy one," she said.

"Sorry. We're getting everything ready. It's going to be . . ."

"Lovely," said Ella.

"Yes. Lovely." I tried to make a joke. "It hardly looks like you need a ceremony."

"We do," said Orpheus.

"Yes, we do," said Ella Grey. "We have to be married surrounded by my friends, and by the beasts and the birds and the sea and the sun."

"Is there something I should be doing for you?" I asked.

"Something?" laughed Orpheus. "You should do *everything*."

"I mean, do I have duties, as the giver-away of my best friend?"

"Your duty," laughed Ella, "is to have the happiest day of your bliddy life."

"Of *my* life."

"Yes. Then you'll be as happy as me. Say you will. Say it fast. Say it true."

"Yes," I told her. "Yes, I will."

"Excellent."

She reached out and caught my arm as I made to turn away.

"And will you love me always, Claire?"

She held me tight on the threshold of her tent.

"Will you? Say yes, Claire!" she hissed. "Say it fast."

"Yes," I whispered into her ear.

"Say it again!"

"I will love you forever, Ella Grey."

"And you will never abandon me."

"I will never abandon you. I am yours, Ella Grey, until the very end of time."

"Good," she said.

"Good," said Orpheus. "Until the end of time. That is what you must say."

And then he leaned past Ella and kissed me, too.

"Thank you," he said.

"For what?"

He grinned, and he seemed suddenly shy, and again he looked just like any boy, like Sam, like James, like Michael; like any boy caught in the delightful trouble of growing up.

"For Ella," he said. "For bringing us together, Claire."

Thud.

"Happy Wedding Day," I said.

"Happy Wedding Day, Claire," said Ella.

Thud, went my heart. *Thud. Thud.*

I put my dinner jacket, dress, yellow shoes and black hat on. The others dressed themselves as well.

We waited on the shore, and then they came hand-in-hand from the dunes. Orpheus wore a loose pale blue shirt, blue jeans. He held the lyre in his hand. Ella was barefooted, wore her Biba dress and had pink flowers tangled in her hair.

The sun shone on them more brightly than it did on us.

Their faces glowed, golden.

"Something else," said Angeline.

"So bliddy *gone*," said James.

Angeline took one of her dolphin earrings out and put it into Ella's ear.

Then we all stood around them, and were strangely awkward with them.

Ella laughed.

"Do you need us to tell you what to do?" she said.

No one answered.

"Make some music first!" she said.

Angeline started to play. James played a whistle, Maria a tambourine. I knocked stones together, Michael whirled dry kelp.

"And have a dance!"

We danced. I danced wildly, kicking the sand, dancing through the edge of the water and dancing back again. I wanted to lose myself in the dance, to forget myself, to forget everything. My heart quickened, quickened.

Thud thud thud

Thud thud thud.

Ella brought me out of it. She took my arm and laughed.

"Calm down," she said. "It's time."

Orpheus was already at the altar, at the centre of the ring of stones. He faced the sea, the islands, the sky.

The sunlight silhouetted him, blazed through his hair.

Ella squeezed my hand. She was very still.

"I'm ready," she whispered.

I couldn't move.

"Lead me to the altar, Claire," she whispered. "And put my hand in his."

There must be something I should say, some advice, some congratulation, some warning. I started to blurt out something, I didn't know what.

"Are you certain . . ." I started.

She put her finger to my lips.

"Just take my hand," she whispered. "Lead me to him."

I took her hand. I hesitated for a final moment, then I led her the short distance through the brilliant Northern light across the soft sand of this lovely beach in the far-flung North of England.

I stepped into the circle of stones and to the altar.

The others stopped their music and watched in silence.

Silence from Bianca and her friends.

Silence also from the sea, the birds, the air.

Silence, it seemed, from the whole wide world.

He didn't turn until we were right behind him.

"Put my hand in his," said Ella.

I did this, and he folded his hand around hers, and he turned.

"Ask if he accepts me."

"Do you," I asked, "accept my friend, the good Ella?"

"I do," he answered, and he sighed, and smiled, as if his whole life had been moving towards this moment.

"Now ask me if I accept him," she told me.

"Do you, Ella, accept Orpheus?"

"Oh, yes I do. Of course I do."

She caught her breath.

"And now, Claire," she said. "Tell us we're wed. Do it fast."

I took a breath and then I whispered,

"I pronounce you . . . wed."

"And tell us we can kiss."

"You may kiss," I said.

They smiled. They kissed. She giggled.

"It's done!" said Ella.

"It's done!" cried Orpheus.

The birds began to sing again, the sea to roar, the breeze to blow.

Sam threw his *Paradise Lost* confetti across their heads.

"Crack the beer open!" said Michael.

"Get the champers from the sea!" said Maria.

"Let's celebrate!" said Ella.

We drank, ate cake, played music, sang and danced. The sun intensified. We ripped off jeans, frocks, dinner jackets, boots and hats and scattered them beside the jetsam. We played our music hard. We yelled in rhythm with it and with our thumping hearts. We threw away all thoughts of home, of the world we'd left behind. We entered Italy, Greece, our transformed selves, the transfigured North.

I danced with Ella in my arms, like the time we danced beneath the gathering stars such a short time ago.

"I love you, Claire," she said. "Thank you for everything. Without you . . ."

"Shh," I whispered.

I put my finger to her lips.

Then Orpheus took the lyre from his back.

ELEVEN

Orpheus sang and played. Northumberland was Greece. The sun blazed down, grew warmer, warmed the sand and warmed our skin. It shone onto the sea and made it azure. It shone onto white birds and made them glitter, onto the dark and made them gleam. Orpheus sat on the sand and played and sang. Ella leaned against him. Red-lipped black-eyed James and bare-breasted snake-wrapped Bianca sat before him. Then we others, a little further back. The music played Orpheus, played all of us and played the world. Sand drifted down from the dunes to hear him. The marram grass tilted to him. Birds came down and the seals came up and crabs crawled from their pools. Porpoises rolled in the turning surf and dolphins danced. From their hiding-places in the dunes, the adders slithered out and slithered out. Did even the rocks roll closer? Did the altar move? Did the sea creep higher than it ever had before?

The music moved our bodies and we danced. We felt it thrumming in our chests and throats. We felt it flowing in and out with breath. We felt it running with our blood. We felt it scattering our thoughts. We felt it annihilating us, turning us from individuals to one thing, one single group, turning this bunch of Tyneside kids into a single being in which we existed with birds and crabs and snakes and dolphins, a single being that blended with sea and sand and sky, a single being with Orpheus at the heart. And it went on and on and on and on. Simple music from a simple lyre and a youthful voice on a Northern beach. Simple music that came from the furthest places of the universe, the depths of time, from the darkest unknown recesses of ourselves. It was the song of everything, all life, all love, all creation. It was his song for my friend Ella Grey.

And then he stopped. Just stopped, just like he did in the kitchen that day. He lowered the lyre. He seemed to stagger and to reel. He looked at us all and seemed amazed that we were there. He whispered into Ella's ear. And then walked through us. Kept his eyes downcast. Went alone, climbing up into the dunes with his blue clothes flowing.

"What was *that*?" said Bianca, coming out from the enchantment.

"Hell's damn teeth," said James.

"Ding dang bliddy dong," said Crystal Carr.

"But why's he stopped?" we asked.

"Where's he gone?"

"Over there, look."

"Ah, yes. There's his head above the grass."

"Yes. There and there."

"What did he say?" asked Angeline.

"Just that he'd be back," said Ella. She laughed. "He's always wandering away."

She picked up a mug of Tesco fizz and swigged from it.

"You can't make music like that," she said, "and come straight back down to earth again."

She hummed some of the melodies he'd played.

"Can you imagine what it must feel like," she said.

She stood on tiptoe, looked inland.

"We'll leave him for a while," she said. "I'll go to find him if he's not back soon."

The sea turned and splashed behind us.

"He's not really made for this kind of thing," she continued. "He doesn't . . . socialize too well."

A black jet fighter streaked low across the horizon.

"You'll understand," she said, "once you get to know him better."

She gazed towards the dunes, the Cheviots behind the dunes, the sky above the Cheviots.

"Orpheus!" she called softly.

No answer, just the turning of the sea, the calling of the birds, the muted roar of another distant jet.

"Play something for us, Angeline," she said.

"OK."

Angeline played sweet music. No birds flew down.

"I'll go and have a look," said Ella. "Shall I?"

"I'll come with you," I said.

She laughed at me.

"He's *my* husband," she said.

"Be back soon," she said.

She ran alone barefooted into the dunes.

I let her run barefooted into the dunes.

A few short moments passed, and then we heard the first scream, then the second, then the third.

We found her surrounded by the slither marks of snakes.

TWELVE

There were tiny bulbs of blood on the tiny bite marks on her ankles. Tiny tiny tiny things. I bent down to them and sucked and spat, sucked and spat. There was hardly a taste from them, just a tiny touch of bitterness, hardly anything at all. Sam dragged her from me, lifted her into his arms and ran. He ran along the jetsam line. He floundered on the soft sand, so he ran through the turning edge of the sea and the water danced and glittered at his feet. Maria and Michael and Angeline and I followed. We couldn't keep up with him. All of our phones were dead, no power in them. We kept clicking them anyway, snarling at them, glaring at them. Somebody, who might have been me and might have been all of us, kept calling,

"Help! Help! Bliddy help! Ella! Ella!"

There were families and walkers on the beach below the castle. They turned to us in dread.

"Snakes!" yelled James. "The snakes got Ella!"

The watchers wore shocked faces, round mouths, furrowed eyes, like masked actors in some ancient play. We ran through the lengthening shadow beneath the castle. Sam slowed, churning his way inland through soft sand again. He gasped and wept. We caught up with him and tried to help, going in close to take her legs to try to share the weight, but she dangled like a dead thing, and trying to help just made it worse.

"She's stopped breathing," Sam gasped.

He found new energy, ran up the black road of The Wynding towards the village.

"She's gone!" he gasped.

I stumbled at his side. I kept reaching to her, trying to touch her heart. I touched the tiny tiny bite marks.

"They're just adders," I said. "They can't kill. She'll be safe. Ella! Oh, Ella!"

"Help! Help!" we cried.

"Ella! Ella!"

"Don't die!" I screamed into her ear. "Don't bliddy die, Ella Grey!"

Where to go to? There were hotels, cafés, a church, a gift shop, a butcher's shop, a gallery. We just stumbled into the green at the heart of it all and yelled like bairns.

"Help! The snakes have killed our friend!"

We laid her down on the grass as they came out from the buildings towards us, as they paused in their early-summer Bamburgh walks. There we were, a bunch of kids, half-naked, with the body beside us in the grass, not knowing what to do, not knowing anything.

And then the policeman, hurrying through the watchers. The policeman from the time before, our friend.

"The snakes have killed Ella!" we gasped at him.

"They can't have," he told us, as he touched her throat, as he felt her wrist, as he touched the bites. "Not the adders. Yes, they'll bite, and yes, they'll cause you pain and yes, they'll cause you sickness for a little time. But kill? No. Never." He leaned right over her. "Or very very rarely," he whispered. "I'm sure she'll be fine." He gave the kiss of life, tried to breathe life into her. "I'm sure she'll be fine," he gasped. He tried again, again. He took out his phone. He trembled as he spoke into it.

"They say it was snakes but mebbe it was something else. No, there's no response from her. No . . . I tried that. No . . . Hurry. Hurry!"

I shoved past him. I opened her mouth with my fingers. I breathed right into her, breathed right into her, tried to breathe my own life into her, tried to call her back from death.

I yelled right into her open mouth.

"Ella! Ella! Ella!"

They were gathered all around us on the green. A dozen, two dozen, three dozen folk.

We heard the siren from the road that runs beside the coast.

"Don't go!" I yelled at her. "Don't leave me, Ella Grey!"

Then here was Orpheus, coming through the folk.

He shoved me away. He leaned over her, and he breathed like I had into her open mouth, he sang a desperate song down into her deepest darkest depths.

"Ella! Ella! Ella Grey!"

He knelt and played his lyre. He leaned over her, bared his teeth at her, as if he wanted to force the music right into her.

"Come back!" he yelled. "Come back to me!"

Then the ambulance was there, and two green-clothed medics came, a woman and a man, and pushed Orpheus aside.

"Not here, son!" they said, as if he were a little child.

The woman took her pulse and checked her breath and breathed into her mouth. The man compressed her chest again, again. He cut open her wedding dress, opened a box, took out a machine, told us to keep back.

He pressed electrodes to her skin. Ella jerked and jumped. She jerked again.

They lifted her onto a stretcher, carried her into the ambulance.

They let me climb in beside her, let me hold her cold hand.

As the doors closed, I saw Orpheus, sprinting like a scared beast back towards the beach.

THIRTEEN

"She told us she'd be fine," said Mrs. Grey.

"And there'd be no trouble," said her husband, "as long as you were there."

"Claire's the best of friends, she said. And the others are lovely, sensible . . ."

"Civilised, she said."

"And us, *we* were so backward."

"*We* were from the Dark Ages."

"Not like other parents."

"Not like other more advanced and modern parents."

"So we relented."

"We let her go."

"We let her go and so she died."

They stood in our kitchen, just inside the back door. The African masks and the Picasso print hung close by them. Mum heard them, and came to them. No, they said, they wouldn't sit. They wanted no tea. No, no wine.

"We're devastated," said Mum. "We loved her so very much."

"She was like another daughter," said Dad, who came in, too.

"She told us that," said Mrs. Grey.

"*They* understand me," said her husband. "*They* know who I am."

They wore grey clothes and their faces were grey.

"She didn't mean it," said Mum. "That's just how children are."

"And you loved her, she knew that," said Dad.

"Love?" said Mrs. Grey. "It was more than love. We gave her *everything*."

"Of course," he answered and he lowered his eyes.

"Of *course*," echoed Mrs. Grey, and I saw that she hated us all.

"The boy," said Mr. Grey. "Of course she told us nothing about the boy."

"You knew, of course," said his wife to me.

"Yes," I answered.

"This so-called singer, this vagabond. This . . ."

"He was unusual," said Dad, "but there seemed nothing bad in him."

Both of them flinched.

"What?" said Mrs. Grey. "You mean you *met* him?"

"Just once," said Dad.

"He was *here*?"

"Yes," said Mum.

"He sat at this table? With Ella?"

"We saw how much he loved her, Mrs. Grey."

"Ah, that thing called love again! So *you* loved her like a best friend, and *you* loved her like a daughter, and you all saw how this wastrel loved her too, and you told us nothing, and you fed him and watered him, and you let him lead her to her *death*?"

"It wasn't like that," whispered Mum.

"No? Is this what your idea of love is? That it involves secrets and lies and ends in death? What about the love that *we* had for her? What about the love that would have protected her and kept her safe?"

"We're sorry," said Dad. "We know now that we should perhaps have told you."

"Ha! And *you*," said Mr. Grey, baring his teeth at me now. "What did *you* do to protect her? What did *you* do, oh best of friends?"

"It was an accident," I answered. "It was a chance in a million. It was the snakes."

"It was no accident," said Mrs. Grey. "It was not the snakes. It was you and you and you, and the rest of the stupid motley crew. You are the ones who caused the death of Ella Grey."

FOURTEEN

The funeral was at the cold grey St. Thomas' Church on Sandoe Street above the Tyne. The air was still, the sky was grey, the river was grey, the sea was grey on the bleak horizon. No birds sang. The church was packed: kids from school, teachers, neighbours, voyeurs drawn by the tale of the death of one so young. A couple of seedy reporters from the *Chronicle* and the *Gazette,* which had told the tale of the tragedy on Bamburgh Beach. There were grey suits, black ties, grey frocks all around us. We bereaved friends sat close together at the back. We wore our vintage, our flowers, our coloured Doc Martens, as Ella would have wished. Bianca and Carlo and Crystal Carr were near the front.

There was no Orpheus.

The Greys were in the front row on their own. Ella's coffin rested on stilts at their side. There were groaning hymns, dirges, gruesome prayers. We didn't know the words, we grunted almost-words along with the dire organ.

The Lord's our uhuhuh,

We'll uh hu.

He lee-eeuh uh to uh.

Mrs. Grey stood on the altar and tried to speak, but she was overtaken by grief. Her husband went to her side and gazed out at us.

"Ella was the best of all daughters," he said. "She was taken from us far too early. But she lives on within us. We shall always be blessed by the time she spent with us. She will shine always within us, our star called Ella Grey."

The priest told us that all things that live must die. He told us that Ella had lived a good life. A place in Heaven had surely been prepared for her. He told us that we would all meet again in glory. He led us in a final dreadful hymn that groaned through the incense-scented heavy air and echoed on the dull church walls.

Black-suited men carried her out and drove her to the graveyard at North Shields. The earth was open, waiting for her to arrive. They lowered her in. More prayers. The priest splashed holy water down onto her. He scattered a handful of soil onto her. The sobbing Greys did the same.

Then they and many other mourners left.

The air hardly moved. A fine drizzle fell. I stayed a while. I stood above the grave.

I wanted to leap down, smash the coffin open, haul her back.

Soon the gravediggers were at their work, shovelling great spadefuls of black earth onto her, shutting her in.

I hated it all. I cursed it all.

Death. Stupid Death.

Come back, Ella Grey!

FIFTEEN

Orpheus? No one knew where he had gone. Hadn't been seen since he ran off that day at Bamburgh.

It's grief, some said.

It's guilt. He's the one who charmed her. He's the one she followed into the dunes.

None of that. It's simply that he'd never bliddy cared at all.

What do you expect? A bloke like that. A waster like that.

He never loved her. How can he have loved her if he left her like this?

Not even at the funeral. Not even at the bliddy grave.

I lay awake at night and wept.

Ella. I wouldn't have left you. I wouldn't have made you follow me barefooted into the dunes. I would have kept you at my side. I would have loved you always.

Where are you now? I whispered into the senseless dark. *Ella, my love! Where are you now?*

And time passed and time passed and nothing healed. The horror didn't diminish, nor the guilt, the pain, the grief.

Then he came, out of the blue. He turned up at our door, on a Saturday afternoon. Stood there in the coat, the boots, the lyre on his back, the grey river and grey sunless sky beyond.

"Where have you been?" I said.

"Everywhere."

My mother called from inside the house.

"Who is it, love?"

"Nobody!" I yelled.

I clenched my fists. I wanted to lash out at him, thump him, crush him, make him bleed, break his bones, make him feel the pain that I felt.

"Why weren't you *here*?" I said.

"I've been searching."

"Searching?"

"Graveyards and churches. Caves and tunnels. Potholes and mines."

"Searching for *what*?"

"Ripping open cracks in the earth. Goggling into gutters and drains."

"Searching for bliddy *what*?"

"For *her,* of course."

"For *who?*"

"For Ella Grey."

Jesus. He *meant* it. He was mad, he'd always been mad. I'd led Ella to a madman.

"Ella's dead," I hissed. "She's in the earth."

"I'm going to follow her."

"What?"

"I'm going to find her."

"Oh, Orpheus."

"I'm going to go to Death and bring her back."

I groaned. But now I saw the depths of his pain. I reached to him. I touched his arm.

His madness was grief. It was the madness of anyone who's lost someone, who can't believe they've gone forever, who can't believe they won't come back.

And I shared the madness. I couldn't believe that my Ella was gone. I couldn't believe that I'd never see her lovely face again, never feel her touch, never hear her voice.

I put my arms around him and we wept.

"I can't go on," he said. "I can't live without her."

"I know," I sobbed. "Oh, I know. I know."

"Will you help me, Claire?" he whispered.

SIXTEEN

I shut the door and we went down towards the Tyne. It flowed and swirled and the breezes blew. We walked by the sites of ancient shipyards, over the cracks in the earth caused by ancient mines. We walked by the places where Ella and I had walked as children. I showed him the place where we washed our dolls together, where we played and splashed together. I saw myself as a girl in the places that I pointed to. I saw Ella as she was. It was like being in a place of ghosts, and one of the ghosts was me.

The day was as grey as the funeral day. There were foghorns out at sea.

"I was wrong," he said. "I was looking in the wrong places."

He crouched. He touched the petals of a daisy by the concrete path.

"Sweet thing," he said.

He smelt his fingers. A beetle was crawling on them. He breathed on it and let it crawl back to the earth.

A blackbird sang. He turned his face to it and smiled, and sang quickly back in answer.

"I found nothing," he said. "I thought I would have to kill myself."

A sudden flock of pigeons swooped over our heads. He made a noise of feathers with his breath and tongue. He made more birdsong and more birds came. He made a sound of water and two salmon leapt.

"Then I knew I had to come back here," he said.

He blew an echo of the breeze. And the breeze blew warm. The clouds were opening, preparing for an astounding dusk, and twin beams of brilliant light shone down through them onto the city.

"I knew I'd have to start from here," he said. "Where it all started."

We walked on, to where the Ouseburn meets the Tyne. We continued alongside the stream towards Seven Stories and The Cluny.

The day was darkening as we came to the slope of grass above the stream. There was music coming from The Cluny, the delighted screams of children from Seven Stories.

"This is the place, Claire," he said. "Tell me about it."

I led him down and we splashed through the water

to the humming gates, to the rattling bolts and locks, the water rushing over us. Time flowed. Darkness thickened all around and the Tyneside night came on. I told the tales of when Ella and I were bairns. I told him what I knew, what I could remember. I told him of the joys we shared, the fears we ran from. I told him of our sleepovers, the many nights we lay together sharing dreams. I knew he must have known it all, but he said he needed to be told it all again, by me, in this place. He plucked the lyre and drew words out of me like song. I went back to the time before I knew her. I told him about the adoption, the Greys. I told him about the baby in the box on the hospital steps.

"And before that?" he asked.

"No one knows. All she had were dreams."

"Dreams?"

"The kind of dreams that any of us can have. Darkness, voices, water."

"Darkness, water, voices," he said. He peered through the gates. "Like this place."

"Yes. We looked through the gates together and saw monsters. We stood by the gates and listened to them sing. We felt water running over us like song."

He lowered the lyre, stooped down, let the water rush through his fingers, let the night deepen around us.

"I need to be alone now," he said.

"What will you . . . ?"

"This is the place," he said. "This is Death's entrance."

He put a finger to my lips.

"If you want her back, you have to leave me."

I couldn't move, couldn't speak.

I stared into the dark.

I wanted to rattle the gates and scream through them.

"Ella," I breathed. "Ella!"

"No more words," he said. "Go home, Claire. Go to sleep. Leave me alone. Don't look back."

PART FOUR

ONE

And how do I go forward now? How do I tell what Orpheus did that night? I wasn't there. I left him, I didn't turn back. I walked through the shadows beneath the moon and beneath the city's golden glow. I went home to whisper Ella's name into the night. To enter a night of weird dreams in which time was all disjointed. I heard Ella calling, calling, calling. I ran to her and found her as a baby lying in a basket. I lifted her out and cuddled her and she giggled and whispered, See? It's all right, Claire! I've decided to start it all again. Then she was a grown-up woman and she held me in her arms, and I looked up into her lovely face and she touched my cheek and soothed me like a mother, murmuring, There there, my love. Don't cry. And there were sudden dreams that were formless, that lurched from my heart and throbbed in my brain and battered my bones. Dreams that were just gulfs of nothingness into which I fell and kept on falling for fragments of eternity. And dreams that rocked me on the bed as if the bed was a boat on an anguished sea. And sometimes there was singing, tiny, tiny, far away. It was the voice of Orpheus, coming and going, growing and fading, diminished by distance, battered by pain and winds and thrashing seas. A lovely note, so far away, coming and going all night long, a note of deepest love, profoundest yearning, unreachable.

And then a final desolate cry of pain.

I woke at last and staggered out into the new day. Nobody else in the house was awake. It was very early, not much after dawn. Sun just daring to peep above the sea. I walked, stumbled towards this sun, and back towards the Ouseburn.

Not a soul to be seen on the pathways, on the riverbanks.

I didn't feel like me, like Claire.

I didn't feel like anyone, like anything.

Orpheus lay in the water against the gates. I clambered down the steel steps towards him. The water made its weird gushing music as it hurried through the gates, and over him, and over his lyre. I waded ankle-deep to him. Rats scuttled away through the gates as I approached him. He was breathing, gulping air and water.

"Orpheus," I whispered. "Orpheus!"

He looked at me as if I were a ghost.

"It's me," I said. "It's Claire."

"What?" he groaned.

"Claire."

"No!" he cried. "No!"

"Come out of the water, Orpheus."

He clutched the bars of the gate and shook them.

"It's me," I said again. "It's Claire."

'What do you see?" he said. "In there! In there!"

I looked into the watery darkness.

"Water, the arches, the shadows, nothing . . . Come out of the water, Orpheus."

"Nothing. No, nothing. That's right."

He let me guide him to the bank. We clambered up to the slope of grass. He cast his gaze around the place: The Cluny, the bridges, Seven Stories, the ever-onward-flowing Ouseburn, the morning sky, the sun.

"This is Hell," he hissed.

I picked away the fragments of Ouseburn litter from his clothes and skin. His clothes were sopping wet. I touched his cheek where his tears and the river water mingled.

"What can I do, Orpheus?" I asked.

"Ha!" he cried softly. "Start again, Claire. Live a

different life. Be born again in another body in another place!"

He sighed at the uselessness of it all.

"And don't hold out the phone," he whispered.

"What?"

"This is what it was all heading for, Claire. Right from the day you held that phone out to me. No way to stop it once it started."

I shook my head, was glad I couldn't speak.

"I almost had her!" he gasped. "She was right behind me, she was almost here!"

He shielded his eyes from the sun with his hands.

"Too much light!" he groaned.

He plucked the lyre. A low dark note, a high and sweet one.

"I found Death," he said. "And I found her, and I almost brought her back."

He plucked the strings again and whispered, sang and told the tale.

"I'll tell it fast and true," he said, "I'll get it out, then I'll be gone."

It's the tale that I must tell as well.

But how to tell such a tale that fits with nothing in the world we know? How to tell a tale that's nothing to do with modern young people like me, like you?

Go back to the start, Claire. Find the entrance to this part of the tale.

Go back to being a child. Tell it as a child would, as we did as children all those years ago, when we put on masks and became other than ourselves, when we became deer, mice, babies, old men, goblins, aliens, so that we could tell our tales more easily.

I'll make a mask.

I'll disappear.

I'll put on a mask, and let Orpheus breathe through me, speak through me.

I'll make the mask of Orpheus and let him sing his tale through me.

TWO

Now, in this house on the banks of the Tyne in the depths of the night, I open the cupboard that's been in my room as long as I know. I shine a little torch into it. I reach into its depths, past soft toys and long abandoned dolls, forgotten games, and crumpled popup books and picture books, past little plastic beasts and jars of beads and fairies' wings.

Here's that box I put away a hundred years ago.

The ancient art-and-craft box: sheets of construction paper, balls of yarn, tubes of paint, brushes, tube of glue, little blue plastic stapler, little red plastic scissors.

I lay them on the little table by the window.

Take a breath, and now begin.

Draw the outline of a head on the card. Cut it out.

Now the mouth, as round and perfect as you can, round as the earth, the sun, the moon. Big enough to sing out songs of joy and howls of awe and to gulp in gasps of fright.

Now the eyes. Make them big and wide to see into the depths of dark.

Wrench the tops of the paint tubes off. Squeeze paint onto this plastic tray.

Soften the brushes.

Paint the face marble-pale.

Outline the mouth in vivid red.

Edge the eyes in black just like the eyes of Orpheus are.

Now the yarn. Choose the black. Cut it to length. Wrench the top of the glue tube off. Spread a film of glue over the top of the head. Arrange the yarn into the hair of Orpheus and stick it there. Let it fall in waves, like the hair of Orpheus does.

Hold the mask to your face and look through the eyes and breathe through the mouth.

Begin to disappear.

Begin to feel like Orpheus.

Now take more yarn, long enough to fasten the mask to your head. Staple the ends of the yarn to the edges of the mask. Pull the mask down over your face and let it stay there, just as you did all those years ago, when you became not-you, when you said that you were gone, when you made yourself anew.

Breathe the air of the night through the wide-open mouth.

Gaze into the dark of the night through the wide-open eyes.

And disappear, Claire Wilkinson. You are no more.

There is only the mask and Orpheus speaking through the mask.

Claire Wilkinson, be gone.

Let Orpheus speak.

Say I am Orpheus.

I am Orpheus.

Begone, Claire Wilkinson.

Again.

I am Orpheus.

I . . .

I . . . am . . .

THREE

I am the one with the coat and the hair and the ancient lyre.

I am the one who can't be still, who comes and goes, the one who looks away, the one who stays a little while then leaves.

I'm the one who sings, always and everywhere.

I met Ella through a mobile phone, but I knew her always and loved her always. I turned up outside school and brought her out. I married her on Bamburgh Beach. She was taken away the very same day on the very same beach.

I know how close love is to death.

I know that joy's twin sister is despair.

Yes, I wept, of course I did, but what's the good of tears? They drown the dead and keep them dead.

I did what I do.

I sang.

Song opens anything.

I'm the one who tames the beasts, who brings the birds down from the sky, who makes the water flow uphill. I'm the one who sang my way through darkness down to Death to bring her back again.

You don't believe me?

Then listen.

Let me speak.

Let me bliddy sing.

The one called Claire, she never truly understood. Why should she? I was the intruder, the trouble, the thief. I came to take her love away. And then I lost her. Stupid, careless Orpheus. But I knew there'd be a way to find our love again. And Claire showed me where my journey had to start. She took me to the Ouseburn gates. She took me back to Ella as a bairn, Ella as a babe, Ella in the dreams of the time before she was a babe.

Where better to find the route to Death than through the gate of life?

That's the gate. That's where all the proper journeys start. Be gone, Claire, I said to her. Go home and sleep and lose yourself in dreams, and leave me here to lament.

I watched her go and darkness fell. I stood in the swirling Ouseburn stream and knew what I must do that night. Aye I trembled, aye I shook and aye I was filled with dread.

Be brave, Orpheus, I told myself. Felt the water singin' over me. Opened my gob and sang along with it, made my song all watery.

Simple sounds, simple tunes.

Gurgles and trickles and splashes and drips.

I plucked the lyre and the strings hummed like the gates of the Ouseburn hummed.

Hear them. Hmmmmmmmm.

I sang my song against the water's flow. Sent my music back to where the water came from. Sang my sounds into the dark beyond the gates.

Tek me in! I sang.

Let me through!

Pressed me lips to the space between the bars.

Separate! I sang.

Break apart and let me through!

I'm Orpheus.

Open, locks!

Separate, bars!

Slide, you bliddy bolts!

Welcome me, Darkness!

Take me, Death!

Oh, let me in!

Who knows how long I stood there? Did anybody see?
Did anybody know? Mebbe they did and they ran in
fright from the singing shadow at the gates. Mebbe they
heard and knew just weird yowling. Mebbe they did and
were entranced, like the rats that gathered around my
feet were entranced, like the cats on the bank that didn't
chase the rats, and the dogs that forgot to chase the cats.
They were as enchanted as this water was. It slowed in
its flowing. It didn't want to leave me and flow into the
Tyne and to the sea. The water deepened around me,
banked up like water's not supposed to bank up round

my calves and feet. I stopped the flowing of the stream with song. It paused to listen to the song of Orpheus.
Did even the moon come down?
Did even the stars move closer?
I didn't know what words I sang, but I knew what their meaning was.

Open up and let me through!

Let me in!

Some would have battered at the gates. Some would have found a way to tear them down. Orpheus just sang. Sang more sweetly and more yearningly than ever he had before.

Open, ye gates! Slide, ye bolts! Open, locks!

Separate, you bliddy bars!

Oh, open gates and let me in!

Now! Oh, please do as I ask!

I'm on my knees.

Oh please! Oh now!

And Oh!

...ends and monsters all around, and plenty of ghosts. But they're such puny things. Mebbe they've been put in here by the dreams of little bairns. Mebbe they're the weird shifting things that Claire and Ella saw all those years ago. Can't make them properly out. They slink in the shadows. They yelp and curse in daft efforts to scare. They shout from cracks in the wall.

From the offshoots of the tunnels.

From the sounds that the water makes.

Just laugh, Orpheus.

These aren't the beasts I've come to overcome.

They threaten nowt. They know nowt. They're the ones that's scared. Funny little frail things. They even bring some comfort. They give Orpheus the chance to practise the songs and noises and echoes and enchantments that will cast their spells down here.

The darkness darkens, the useless monsters call, and Orpheus wades on.

The city's all above me as I walk, the city with its homes and offices, its roads. Its churches, ha! Its schools! Ha! The civilized world. Its work and habits and safe routines. Its people tucked up safe in bed, telling tales to each other to tame the night. Its people loving each other as darkness deepens. Then sleep that fills the night with cries and groans and murmurs and snores.

And infants dream of monsters, the young dream dreams of love, the old dream dreams of being young.

Do some of the young dream of snakes on dunes?

Do they dream of what's happening now below, of Orpheus looking for Ella? Mebbe it's Claire who dreams this dream, Orpheus wading through this darkness towards Death.

Dream, Claire.

I carry your love.

I sing the journey to Ella Grey.

I sing the way to Death and Re-Creation.

The tunnel twists and climbs and dives and curves, and darkness darkens, darkens, darkens. Nowt grows down here, of course. No birds, no spiders, no beetles, no flies. Nowt swims nor slithers around my feet. Even the rats have scattered and gone.

There's stones from ancient homes, skeletons of ancient dead, fossils of forgotten beasts, seams of ancient coal.

I walk and wade alone, go deeper, darker.

And who are these now, these little pale ones? Oh, they're bairns. A scattered bunch of little bairns. Don't they see me? They're wading their way back to the gates but getting nowhere. Their forward-moving toddling footsteps just move them backwards, into the deeper dark. In reaching for the light, they're being overwhelmed by dark. Oh, I see. They don't understand. They don't know they're dead. I hesitate. I move towards them, but what's to say to them?

I say nowt. I sing to them, lullabies and nursery songs and sounds made by mothers and fathers. But then I stop. This just reminds them all of what's been lost. Nothing to do.

I turn away from them at last. Mebbe in Death it's up to the dead to know what they are and why they're here. But how hard this is for the lost little ones who had such a short time in the light. Will anybody love them, here? Will anybody care for them, down here?

Just move on, Orpheus.

Keep on moving, wading, all alone, into the deeper dark. And now there's others. They lean against the curving walls, hunch in the water, trudge painfully against the water's flow. These are the ones who know their fate. These are the ones who know there's no way back.

Do they see me? Mebbe they do and they think I'm just another of the ordinary dead.

I move on past them, singing.

I'm the one living thing in the crowd of the dead.

Orpheus, the singer.

Orpheus, with his lyre.

Orpheus, the first ever to come here in order to come out again.
And now I start to call her name.

"Ella! Ella! Ella Grey!"
No answer.
The trudging dead around me make no noise.
No sound but water, lyre, song.
Then a whisper, so soft I'm not sure that I hear it, so intimate it could have come from deep inside myself.

"TURN BACK, SINGER."

I listen closely to the dark.

"SINGER. YOU MUST TURN BACK."

A woman's whisper, sweet and soft.
Then silence. I walk on.

The shades of the dead are all around me now, shuffling onward.

Don't be scared, Orpheus.

Don't be afraid.

The tunnels start to multiply.

New curves and openings and offshoots appear.

Shafts and walkways leading downward. Sudden

chambers where the music travels far and long before it

echoes back again, where the name of Ella travels far

and long before it echoes back again. Caverns where

water runs down rock and drips from rock.

"Ella! Ella! Ella Grey!"

The voice again, just a fraction more than silence.

"TURN BACK, SINGER. TURN BACK."

Don't be afraid.

Forward.

Downward. I leave the Ouseburn far behind.

Now there's strange breathing all around,

soft groans and growls and wordless whispers.

What's this? More water. Still, or almost still,

it moves across my feet like breath.

Beyond it are distant yowlings,

muttering and murmurings.

I start to wade.

Ankle-deep, shin-deep, knee-deep.

"YOU!"

It's a snarl, a growl, close by.

"WHAT ARE YOU?"

I see eyes, teeth. Some great claw or hand gets me by the shoulder. Hot stinking breath falls across my face.

"WHAT ARE YOU?"

I'm dragged to it. There's hanging hair against my skin, some great limb, quivering muscle.

"SPEAK!" it growls.

It forces me to my knees into the black and icy water. It looms over me in the dark, darkest of shadows with teeth and eyes and yawning jaws.

"SPEAK!"

"I am Orpheus."

"WHAT DO YE THINK YOU'RE DIYING DOON HERE?"

"I lost my love."

It roars with laughter, with contempt.

"YE LOST YER LOVE! OH, POOR THING!"

"Ella Grey. I've come to take her back again."

"HAVE YE NOW? LET US HELP YOU, THEN! OH, ELLA! ELLA GREY! IT'S TIME TO GAN YEM, PET!"

It puts its claws around my throat.

"O LITTLE STUPID LIVING MAN! I'LL TEAR YE LIMB FROM LIMB RIGHT NOW TO BID YE WELCOME. GIVE US THIS ARM, GIVE US THIS LEG, LET US RIP YOU."

feel its teeth on my shoulder. They tighten.

'Let me sing," I gasp.

'SING? AYE, SING
WHILE I RIP YE. SING
WHILE I SUCK YER
MARROW AND SLURP
YER BLOOD. SING AS I
SCATTER YER BITS INTO
THE DEEP POOL OF THE
DEAD."

lean my head away from its jaws and I sing again.
sing low and soft, high and sweet.

t laughs again, it snarls, but softer now

"I'LL RIP OOT YER TONGUE AND CRACK YER SKULL. I'LL CHEW YER SKIN AND CRUNCH YER BONES. I'LL MEK YE LIKE YE SHOULD BE WHEN YE'RE DOON AMONG THE DEAD."

The great teeth gripping, the wet tongue licking, the loose lips drooling.
I sing, I pluck the lyre. The beast, whatever it is, holds me close. Even down in Death, I tell myself, beasts such as this can be calmed.

"What are you?" I ask, in a pause between sweet notes.

"I GUARD THE DEAD. I LET THEM THROUGH. I KEEP THEM DEAD. AND NOBODY BUT THE DEAD CAN PASS."

I sing.
I hear the sighing in its voice.
I feel its muscles starting to relax.

"Let me through," I whisper.

"NA!"

"Please let me through."

"NO. OH, BLIDDY NO."

I sing. I sing. It sighs. It sighs.

At last the jaws relax. It sleeps. It gently snores.
I wade on, past the beast, through the thigh-deep water,
to the darkest dark beyond.
And step up to the dry land beyond. Just bare rock.
Just darkness that might go on forever and forever.
I walk into it, singing.
There are sounds down here apart from mine, but oh
so frail, so distant, as if from a universe away. Who would
have thought that the space beneath the city in the North
could be so immense?
"Ella," I whisper.

"Ella!" I call.

"TURN BACK, SINGER,"

comes the whisper.

"Ella!"

"I SAID TURN BACK."

The woman's voice, close by, so close it could be coming from right inside my ear.

"WHO ARE YOU?" it says again, like the hoot

of an owl in a far-flung night.

"My name is Orpheus," I sing.

"ORPHEUS, GO HOME."

Then darkness, and silence. I listen, I carry on.
Then another whisper, a different, sharper voice.

"SING YER TALE FOR US, ORPHEUS."

And another.

"SING IT OUT, LAD. WE'RE LISTENIN'."

So I start to sing the tale but I've hardly started when there's laughter in the darkness all around.

"STUPID BLIDDY ORPHEUS,"

something whispers.
Then a stream of mocking voices.

"STUPID BLIDDY CRACKPOT SINGER."

"THERE'S NAE SUCH THINGS AS TALES DOON HERE."

"THERE'S JUST THE ENDS OF TALES."

"THE TAILS OF TALES."

"AND ALL THE ENDS IS JUST THE SAME."

"SO ALL TOGETHER NOW!"

"AH, ONE TWO THREE FOUR!"

"AND THEN SHE DIED AND THEN SHE

DIED AND THEN!

AND THEN SHE DIED AND THEN SHE

DIED AND THEN!

AND THEN SHE BLIDDY DIED AND

BLIDDY DIED!"

"THE END! THE E-E-E-E-E END!"

"THE END THE END THE END THE END

THE END.

THE END THE END THE END THE END

THE END.

THE END THE END THE END THE END

THE END.

AND THAT'S THE BLIDDY END OF BLIDDY

THAT!"

"AHA-AHA-AHA-AHA-HAHA

AHA-AHA-AHA-AHBLIDDYHA!"

Take no notice, Orpheus. Sing her name.
Let them cackle all around.

"Ella!"

"SING IT AGAIN!" they laugh and call.

But then they fade.they fade.they fade.they fade.
I walk on into the deepest darkness until I can walk
no more,
can sing no more.

I stand alone.

I'm beyond the shuffling dead, the beasts,
beyond the cackling voices.

An aeon, or a minute, passes.

There is nothing.

Not a movement, not a sound.

Nothing at all.

No way forward, no way back.
No way to howl and yell and gnash my teeth
and yell out, "Please give her back to me!"

Nothing.
Nowt.
Bugger all.

An age passes, or a microsecond.

"WELL DONE, ORPHEUS."

It's the woman's whisper once again, soft, soft, so soft and sweet it's hardly there at all. A sound like the sound made by the finest string of the lyre.

She's so close that if I knew how to reach out and how to touch she'd be right beside me.

"YOU HAVE SUNG YOUR WAY

SO FAR," she says.

"Who are you?"

I hear her smile.

"LONG AGO YOU WOULD HAVE

KNOWN ME."

"AND ME AS WELL."

It's another voice, a man's. And his is the sound made by the heaviest string of the lyre.

"Who are you?" I ask again.

I hear him smile.

"YOU'VE SUNG YOUR WAY INTO THE NOTHING AT THE HEART OF EVERYTHING," he says.

"Who are you?"

They speak the harmony made by the deepest and the sweetest strings.

"WE ARE DEATH, ORPHEUS," they say.

"YOU HAVE REACHED US," they say.

"AND WHAT WILL YOU DO NOW?"
they say.

What can I do? I lift the lyre into the nothingness.
I send its tune and my voice into the void.
I sing the world above. I sing the sun and the earth and
the sea. I sing Northumberland, Bamburgh Beach, waves
rolling onto shining sand. I sing the Farnes stretching
towards the horizon. I sing rolling porpoises, leaping
dolphins, hooting seals, puffins that dash by in coloured
flights, terns that hover and dance in the shimmering air.
Crabs and anemones and little quick fish that seem to
glow. Kelp and bladderwrack and sea snails and urchins.
The damp sand and the dry sand and the line of jetsam
in between. The rocks and rockpools. The breeze that
whispers in the marram grass and whips up spray from
the waves. I sing the snake and the spider and the
scrabbling mouse. I sing yelling children plunging
through surf. I sing running dogs. I sing the castles
children build in sand, the words they write in it, the
shrines they build with rocks and kelp. The distant
Cheviots, the drifting clouds, the heavenly blue of sky.
I sing young people singing. I sing their astonishment
at living in such a place. I sing them praising the world

in all its forms. I sing the failing sun, dusk and darkness coming on, blue sky yellowing, orangeing, reddening. The moments when sea merges with sky and all seems held in air, floating. The first few stars and a sickle moon, and the intensifying beauty of the night. The endless glittering lights that stretch forever into the gulfs of space and time above this little beach. I sing the glow of gold above the city, the turning lighthouse light, the crackle and flames of the fire, the smell of sausages cooking, tomatoes simmering. I sing the taste of all these things, the taste of wine and of clear cool water and salt. I sing the taste of fruit as it fizzes to life on the tongue. And the feel of the air against the skin, the grains of sea salt on it, the grains of sand and the tingle of the day's sun on it. I sing murmuring, whispering outbursts of laughter and affection. I sing young people loving by their fires and in their tents and in the soft folds of the dunes. I sing old people walking hand-in-hand. I sing the world. I sing the world. I sing the world. I sing

Ella,
Ella,
Ella Grey.

"OH, ORPHEUS," whispers Death in harmony
with itself.

"Let me take her back to that," I sing.

Their silence lasts a minute, a day,
a month, a year, an age.

I sing again.

I sing again.

Life,

I sing.

Light,

I sing.

"SHE CAME HOME TO US, ORPHEUS." The woman.

"WE SENT HER OUT AND WELCOMED HER BACK." The man.

"AS WE DO WITH ALL OUR CHILDREN."
"WE ALWAYS LOVED HER, ORPHEUS."
"WE WAITED FOR HER ALL THESE YEARS."

"And I!" I cry. "I loved her and love her still and all I ask is a little more of time with her."

Sighs from both of them:
impossibly sweet, impossibly deep.
"Then she will be yours again, for all eternity, Orpheus."

Together, the woman and the man: *"YES."*
Together, in harmony: *"ELLA! ELLA!"*
I sing with them,
my note perfectly balanced between theirs.

The three-voiced chord sings out.

"Ella!"

"YES!" gasps Death. *"SHE HEARS,
ORPHEUS. AND SHE COMES."*

I'm mad to see. Death restrains me.
*"YOU MUST NOT LOSE HER
AGAIN, ORPHEUS."* The man.

*"YOU CANNOT SEE HER HERE
IN DEATH."* The woman.

*"YOU MUST LEAD HER OUT
TOWARDS THE LIGHT AND
LIFE."*
*"THEN SHE WILL BE YOURS
AGAIN."*

"Ella!" I call.

Then her voice, from the nothingness, the darkness.

"Orpheus!"

Her voice!

"Orpheus!

Orpheus!"

"DON'T LOOK." The man.

"*SHE WILL FOLLOW YOU,*" says Death,

in harmony with itself.

"*BUT YOU CANNOT TURN. YOU MUST NOT SEE HER UNTIL YOU HAVE LED HER OUT INTO THE WORLD AGAIN.*"

I hesitate.

"*YOU HESITATE?*" says Death.

"No."

"*GO NOW.*"

I walk.

"*LEAD HER TO THE LIGHT, ORPHEUS. WALK, WADE, SING. TRUST DEATH. SHE WILL BE*

WITH YOU, ORPHEUS. DON'T LOOK BACK."

"Thank you," I sing.

"NO THANKS UNTIL THE JOURNEY'S DONE. GO NOW."

I walk away. I wade into the knee–deep pool,
and I hear another wading close behind.

"Ella? It's you?"
And her voice!

                      "Yes, Orpheus. I'm with you."

I yearn to see her, to stride hand–in–hand with her.

                      "Don't turn,"
            she whispers, so close behind.

We pass the beast, which still lies stunned
by the beauty of the song.

"Death allows this," I whisper as I pass. "Death says let us through."

The beast growls regretfully. I hear Ella wading past it. We step up onto rock. The cackling voices here are stilled. Just cracked breathing, meaningless vindictive hisses and snorts.

"Ella?" I sing.

"Yes, Orpheus. Yes."

We walk against the endless flow of the subservient shades of the dead.

We pass the reluctant ones, those who haven't yet accepted the inevitability of their fate.

I play music that guides our feet in easy regular rhythms towards the light. One step then another, one step then another, one note then another.

"Oh, poor children!"

I hear Ella sigh, as we pass the little bairns.

"No good," I call back to her. "Smile at them and pity them, but keep on moving on."

Faint glimmerings of light now. Or no.
Am I just deceived by what I most desire?

"Ella!"

"Yes, Orpheus. I'm here."

"Won't it be wonderful?"

"Yes! I'll leave school."

"Will you?"

"And I'll leave the Greys.
I'm old enough. Just let them try to stop me."

"We'll travel together, man and wife."

"Far and wide. Orpheus and Ella."

"Ella and Orpheus."

"We'll make children!"

"Children?"

"Yes! Just imagine that!
The children of Orpheus and Ella!"

"Yes."

"No, Orpheus! Don't look back!"

I don't. I quicken the rhythms and our steps. I move so much more quickly than when I entered. I know the way to life through these turning, twisting, upward-mounting tunnels. Above us is the city, the civilized world. How long has it been asleep? How long have I been away? A microsecond, a million years? Up there, are they waking from a single sleep, or has a new age come, has the city disappeared, has the whole world changed? Has the whole world gone?

Yes, that is light somewhere up ahead.

The tunnels climb towards it.

I hurry, hurry.

"Too fast?" I ask her.

                "No, Orpheus. Oh, look, the light!"

We pass the place of the silly monsters.
I play as I pass them,
turn their noises into song again.

"BOOOOO!
HISSSS.
NANANANA!"

Ella giggles and joins in.

"I know who you are!"
she laughs. "I used to see you when I was a frightened
little lass! Remember me and Claire looking in at you?
Boo!"

I turn my steps into a dance. I let the music twist and
bend and I let my body sway. We're dancing homeward
in the Ouseburn. The rats are back to scuttle at my feet.
I've sung Ella out of Death! I'm dancing Love back
home again!

We're closer,
closer to the light.

And there are the gates. It's morning just beyond them.
The water hums through the gates,
through me, through Ella Grey.

"Hurry!" I call.

"Faster!"

                                        "Don't look back."

I reach the gates. I grab them and laugh.
"Separate!" I sing. "Open, locks! Slide, you bliddy bolts!"
I sing and sing at them.

"Open up and let us out!"
Ella waits, so close behind.
                                        "Oh, let us out!"
                                        she calls.

And Oh! She touches me.

It's just

the

gentlest

of gentle

touches on my shoulder.

And how could anybody not turn at that?
How could anybody not look back from a locked gate
to check they weren't deceived, that their one true love
was there?
Who could have resisted?
Of course it's bliddy her. Of course it is.
And even as I see it's her and even as we reach towards
each other at last, as our eyes meet in desolate joy, she's
already going back. And she's already gone. And I've
been flung out, and I'm right back where I started, on
the wrong side of the gates. And there's just the empty
tunnels leading back to Death, the humming of the metal
bars, the chinking of the bolts and locks, the scrabbling
rats around my feet, the sunshine pouring down on me
and darkness deepening everywhere.
Oh, bliddy stupid Orpheus.
Of course Ella Grey was bliddy there.

FOUR

Take off the mask.

Put it down.

Its job is done.

Be Claire again.

Desolate Claire Wilkinson.

Ella almost came.

She was almost here again.

But Orpheus looked back.

Thud.

FIVE

He told me his story that morning when I found him
lying outside the gates, as the Ouseburn flowed and the
bars rattled and hummed and the light intensified all over
Tyneside. He never once asked if I believed. As he
approached the end of it, his eyes were shifting, looking
towards the cluttered horizon of the city and the austere
horizon of the sea. He wanted to be away. I thought of
questions to detain him but most of them were useless
stupid things.

"She was lovely?" I asked him. "Like she was in life?"

"Yes," he said.

I looked towards the gates and imagined her there at
the edge of the light. I imagined standing at the gates
myself and calling her and calling her.

"If I hadn't handed you the phone that day," I said.
"If I hadn't . . . ?"

He shook his head.

"Oh, Claire. There's no way to talk about it now."

"You could come home with me," I said. "We could have some breakfast . . . We could . . ."

He just smiled, lowered his eyes.

"Do ye really think so, Claire?"

"What will you do?"

"I'll wander. I'll sing. What else can I do?"

"Will I see you again?"

"Maybe ye'll hear me."

We stared at each other, useless, desolate. And he breathed deeply in and then breathed out again.

"Thank you," he softly said.

"For what?"

"For helping me to find her a second time."

He sang his last lament, so bleak, so sad, so beautiful, and it seemed the whole world wept, including me.

"Without you," he told me, "I would never have even known that she existed."

Then he hugged me, and he left. Climbed up the opposite bank with the water of the Ouseburn dripping from him. Didn't look back. Stood for an instant silhouetted against the shimmering sky, then turned northwards and was gone.

PART FIVE

ONE

He busked in Alnwick at the summer fair. He stood
waist-deep in the sea at Lindisfarne, surrounded by seals,
and sang at the sky. He roamed like a tramp in the
Cheviots. He begged for bread at caravan sites, holiday
cottages, farmhouses. He was holed up in a ring of
teepees with hippies in the Simonside Hills. He skulked
in a ruined bastle at Wooler's far end. His songs were
more lovely than ever. They ached with sadness and
longing, they were songs to break the heart. Trees hung
down their branches, drizzle fell, cows and sheep were
seen to cry. No, the truth was that the singer had
turned beastly. He was losing human form. He crawled
on all fours, and yelled out drink- and drug-fuelled
animal howls and yaps and yelps. All living things recoiled
from him.

Or he was further afield. In Greece itself, where he

sang on the steps of the Parthenon and on the slow-moving ferries to the islands. He sang on the beaches of Crete. He sang in Rome, on the Spanish Steps, and in the hills of Tuscany where he followed in the footsteps of St. Francis. He worked as a lounge singer on a cruise liner in the Baltic. He was with a band in New York writing an album of songs. He was rehearsing Monteverdi at La Scala. He was about to appear on *Britain's Got* bliddy *Talent*. He was . . .

All was rumour. Nothing was true. The tales were tittle-tattle for time-wasters, gossip-mongers, little bairns. They blew with the wind, fell with the rain, were sung by blackbirds, cawed by crows, squealed by silly gulls.

And beneath the tales there was just silence. And maybe the true truth was what many said—Orpheus had drowned, he'd slit his wrists, he'd overdosed, Orpheus was dead.

Everything was silent in the winter. We all worked worked worked, preparing for next year's exams. We read our texts and read them again and tried to commit them to our hearts. Those of us who had loved her kept a photograph of smiling Ella in our books. She bookmarked my texts, my notes, my scribblings. She walked through my thoughts, waded through my dreams.

Sometimes I woke in the dead of night and heard wet footsteps in the street outside and heard her calling, *Claire! It's me. They let me out again!* I heard her coming up my stairs, rattling my door. *Open up! Let me out!*

Sometimes I dared to open the door, to discover nothing but the steep dark stairwell with the fading echo of her voice in it.

Snow fell, and deepened, deepened. Temperatures plummeted. Minus 10, minus 15, even here in the city. I thought of Orpheus in such a winter. How would he cope? But he must have always coped. These days I couldn't walk anywhere without imagining the world below. The solid ground was built on nothingness. Every crack was the chink below which the great gulf lay. Every opening was an entrance to the chasms of eternity.

Icicles hung on the Ouseburn gates. Ice thickened on the bars and locks and feathered the edges of the stream. Beyond the gates, in the frosted gloom, the fleeting shapes of familiar demons shifted.

We still gathered at The Cluny. We sat in our circle wrapped in scarves, close together to share our heat. We talked of Italy, Greece, of what we'd do when spring and summer came again. But where was there to go when

Northumberland held the memories of such pain? We talked of places further to the South—Yorkshire, Sussex, Cornwall—but we felt no passion for them. Strange. The beauties of the North seemed to be intensified by the loss we had experienced there, and they drew us back to them. We'd go again, we said. We'd celebrate our lost friend's life there. *And maybe he'll come back again* was what many thought and none dared whisper.

Bianca stopped me in the corridor one day.

"Nae word?" she said.

"Of what?"

"Of him, of course. Of bliddy Orpheus."

I shrugged. I told her no.

"He'll be back," she said.

"Aye," said Crystal Carr, coming up behind her. "That one's too damn fit to just gan dark."

"He's brokenhearted," I said.

"He's a lad," said Crystal.

"And she was just a lass," said Bianca.

"He'll get over it."

"Be back to his senses soon enough."

"And then he'll need a damn good seein' to."

They giggled, leered.

"He knaas what's on offer here."

"Bliddy right. He can tek the two of us."

"Ding dong."

"Ding dang dong."

"Ding dang diddly diddly ding dang dong."

The year turned. The Northern dark relented. We dared to hope for spring. It came slowly, slowly.

Then James came to my side one Monday morning.

"I think I saw him," he said.

"Him?"

"Orpheus."

"When?"

"Yesterday."

"It was really *him*?"

"I'm sure it was."

"Where?"

"I was at Craster. With Paul."

"Paul?"

He blushed.

"My friend," he said. "It was so lovely. Still freezing but the air was like crystal. The sea was bright blue. We were walking on the track to Dunstanburgh, between the beach and the dunes. You know it?"

Yes, I knew. Another lovely northern place, another place to sing about, another place for words and tales.

Yellow sand and black cormorants on black rocks and the jagged ruins of the castle on the headland.

"I couldn't believe it," James went on. "Him. The hair, the coat, the lyre. That's him, I said to Paul. 'Who?' he said. Orpheus, I told him. He's sitting on the beach, some other guys with him. Paul wanted to meet him, of course."

"And you did, too?"

"Yes. So we went down to the sand. The other guys are sitting and standing in a sort of ring around him. I think he's got the lyre in his hands but he's not playing it."

"Just guys, no girls?"

"No girls. They turn round as we step down onto the beach. They bunch up, and you can see they don't want us there. Orpheus turns and sees us. I speak his name: Orpheus. Doesn't seem to recognize me. 'I'm James,' I say. One of the blokes comes close and tells us to shove off. 'Orpheus,' I say again. 'I knew Ella. I was there the day . . .' He looks at me and I'm sure he remembers, but he turns his head away towards the sea. The bloke stands right in front of me. 'Clear off back to where you come from,' he says. 'But I know him,' I say. 'No you don't,' says the bloke. 'You know nothing.' Paul comes to my side. 'I said shove off,' says the bloke. Then another one's

there. I say we don't want any trouble. I call to Orpheus.
I ask him is he OK. He looks again, but he doesn't
respond. 'See,' says the bloke. 'He doesn't know you.
He doesn't want to know you. He wants
you gone.' I don't know what to do. Some of the
blokes look hard as nails: leathers and boots and like
they're just waiting for an excuse to start on us. Or
maybe they were just protecting him. 'Come on,' says
Paul. So we leave. I keep turning back. Orpheus doesn't.
We walk on to Dunstanburgh. I try to tell Paul what it
used to be like, what his music was like, but there's no
way I can tell him, really. When we come back again,
Orpheus and his mates are gone. Just the tracks of them
leading from the sand onto the grass and no sign of them
anywhere."

"It was really him?"

"It was. I'm certain. It must have been . . ."

"It wasn't cause you *wanted* it to be him?"

"No. No."

"He looked OK?"

"Same as he always looked."

"Gorgeous?"

"Gorgeous, like always. And like he nearly wasn't
there, like he didn't really want to be there, like always."

• • •

Sam learned to drive that spring. His parents allowed him to borrow their car. He took me on little jaunts up into the Durham hills, and down to South Shields. Sometimes he pulled up in obscure laybys and we made a clumsy kind of love. He became more confident and one Sunday morning he drove us northwards, across the Tyne, across the coalfields, towards the beaches.

"This is the life," he said, putting his foot down, speeding towards the sea. "Footloose and free," he said. "The world's our bliddy oyster."

He knew I wasn't with him. I made him take me to Craster, to Dunstanburgh, to the road alongside the dunes at Bamburgh. I told him to take me across the causeway to Holy Island. He saw me peering into the world to catch a sight of what we'd lost. Once or twice I saw what I thought was him and called out, "There, Sam! There!" but it was not him.

"Stop it, Claire," Sam said.

"Eh?"

"He's gone, just like she has. And even if he hasn't he wouldn't want you."

I said nothing. A herd of startled cattle ran through a nearby field.

"All he wants these days is lads. Lads like James, that's what the story is."

"Is it, now?"

"Aye, it is. That's the way he's gone."

He glared at me, then accelerated suddenly.

"I'll take you bliddy home," he said.

He drove too fast for the twisting roads leading back towards the A1. At Howick he braked suddenly as a pheasant dawdled in front of us. The car lurched into the roadside hedge. He pressed his face to the steering wheel.

"Go to hell, Claire," he said.

I waited. Thorns and broken twigs and foliage pressed against my window. He went on cursing me, then backed the car out of the hedge. He didn't dare look at the bodywork damage, drove the car carefully away.

There were tears in his eyes. We drove in silence. We got onto the A1 and headed south.

"It's hopeless, isn't it?" he said.

"You care nowt for me, do you?" he said.

"Oh, Sam," I whispered. "Of course I do."

"You think I'm just a fool."

"I don't."

"What's wrong with me, then?"

No answer.

We headed homeward.

"Mebbe you should find another Ella," he said, "and not bother with bliddy lads at all."

Long silence, from both of us.

"Aye," he said. "Mebbe that's the way it should all turn out."

How do stories spread? How fester? How get such momentum? People take the words and spin them. They play with them, polish them, recreate, intensify them, cast them on. The tales flow like water, take new currents, eddies, whirlpools, swirls. They find new routes, flow over new beds, cut new gullies, draw on different sources.

"Gone gay?" said Carlo in the schoolyard one day. "Where's the surprise in that? He was always bliddy gay."

Others rushed into the conversation.

"Always."

"Right from the start."

"So bliddy obvious."

"That coat."

"That lyre."

"That bliddy voice."

"Aye, that voice."

"And the way he stood there singing."

"Oooh, I'm Orpheus."

"Hmmmm. I'm bliddy gorgeous."

"Lalalala just look at me."

"Bliddy Jessie."

Crystal Carr, hands on hips, head tilted. "Bliddy teaser."

"Hahahaha!"

Bianca, pulling her top down. "Must've been gay not to notice this."

Giggles. Giggles.

"Teaser."

"Ha!"

So the mocking song got into the air and into the songs of the birds and the blowing of the wind and the flowing of the water. There was much laughter, many jokes. But they were laced with venom. And the laughter grew in hate.

Teaser. Poser. Trickster. Fooled us all. Fooled poor lost Ella.

"Aye, especially Ella Grey."

"Aye, specially that poor lass."

"And he knew what he was doin'."

"Course he did."

"Dead right."

"Bliddy charmer."

"Bet it's not the first time."

"Bet it's bliddy not."

"Bet there's been tons of bliddy Ella Greys."

"Ella after Ella."

"And there'll be tons more if he's not stopped."

"Teaser."

"Killer."

"Aye, bliddy killer."

"Aye, if he'd not turned up she'd be with us still."

"Killer."

"Murderer."

"He'll get what's comin'."

"We'll find a way to find him."

"He'll get his bliddy dues."

Such venom, such contempt. It seemed out of kilter. Yes, he brought trouble, but he also brought joy, he brought love. There had been nothing like his music in our world before. But all was turning like the tide, like the relentless earth. Admiration turned to scorn. Astonishment to disbelief. Laughter to savagery. Love to hate. And they turned as if they were destined to turn, as if the song of praise that had sung through Orpheus was bound to become a song of hate that sang through them and drove them on. Soon they were talking of searching for him, hunting for him, punishing him.

"We'll give him his comeuppance," they snarled.

"We'll make him pay."

• • •

Spring quickened, strengthened. Unfurling leaves, first blossom, bright yellow daffodils trumpeting above the grass. Exams loomed. We worked harder, harder. All of us were under pressure. Why must we work so hard when the sun blazed through the classroom window and the world was telling us to play? Krakatoa growled, grumbled, urged us on. It would all be for the best, he said. Discipline now would earn us years of freedom later. Don't be distracted. Keep your eyes on the prize.

He erupted one afternoon in late March when Bianca shoved her books aside and groaned.

"Yes, Miss Finch?"

"It is all so bliddy *boring.*"

"Continue."

"It is all so bliddy *ancient.*"

He stood in the aisle among us. He seethed.

"Paradise Lost!" Bianca went on. "Let's all go abliddy Maying, and my ending is despair and blablablablablabla-bla. We've got our lives to live. We're *young!*"

"*Infantile* is perhaps a better word."

"Sod off!" she snarled at him. "*Decrepit* is the word for you. *Knackered* is the word. Worn out! Useless! Bliddy ancient! Look at you, old man!" She stood up. She glared at all of us. "Look at all of you! Old before you let yourselves be bliddy young!"

"Get out," said Krakatoa.

She didn't move. She grinned.

"Get out, you . . ."

"Say it," she sneered. "You've been dying to say it all these months . . ."

"You stupid child. You little tart. You . . ."

She grinned.

"Oh, sir!" she simpered.

"Get out!" he yelled.

She coolly lifted her bag from the back of her chair.

She puckered her lips at him.

"Don't do that!" he snapped.

"Do what, sir?" she asked.

She tilted her head, smoothed her shirt over her breasts.

"Get out!"

He stepped closer to her. His eyes bulged. His face was purple. His fists were clenched.

"Oh, *sir!* " she said. She widened her eyes, licked her lips. "What *are* you going to do, sir?"

He slumped, he groaned.

"Go back," he muttered.

"Back where?"

"To whatever slime you slithered from, you slut . . ."

"Oh! What drives you to such language, sir?"

She licked her lips. She blew a kiss at him.

"Goodbye, old man," she said. "Goodbye to all of you. And go to hell, each and every one of you."

She went out the door. Crystal jumped from her chair and followed her.

Krakatoa closed the door.

"Continue with your work," he muttered.

"Forgive me," he whispered.

"That was not me," he said.

"Oh, ye Gods," he sighed.

We watched the two girls cross the yard just as we had watched Ella all those months ago. They swaggered arm-in-arm into the shimmering emptiness at the edge of the schoolyard.

They didn't turn.

They went beyond our sight towards the story's end.

TWO

This is what she came back with, Bianca, just two weeks later. It was night. There'd been some kind of power cut. I was reading. I was taking time off from revising, trying to move past all the ancient stuff. I shone my torch down onto *The World's Wife,* but could make no sense of anything. I looked out. Great swathes of Tyneside were in deepest black beneath the glittering stars. Dogs were howling. Someone somewhere was screaming: a crazy game or murder, no way to know.

Mum called my name from downstairs.

"Someone to see you!" she called.

I went down and found Bianca standing in the kitchen, in the firelight and candlelight. Skin gleaming, hair awry, dark stains on her clothes, little rucksack on her back. Bianca, all subdued, tattoo on her neck, so out of place among the Le Creuset pots and the prints, like somebody from a different world.

"It's Bianca," said Mum, stupidly.

She widened her eyes at me as she said it.

"She says she's a friend of yours," she said.

"She is."

"From school?"

"Yes," I said.

I touched Bianca's arm.

"Can I get you anything?" I said.

She shook her head.

"No."

"Come on upstairs," I told her.

We went up. I told her to sit on the bed. I asked her nothing. We sat in silence for a long time. Maybe I knew the kind of thing that was on its way.

At last she spread her hands before her, rubbed at the stains on them.

"It's blood," she whispered.

"Still there," she whispered.

She sighed. She reached down into her rucksack and took out a little bottle of vodka. Held it out to me. I shook my head. She unscrewed the cap and swigged.

"I think I loved him," she said.

"Him?"

"Orpheus."

"But the things you've said about him. The things . . ."

"I always did. Right from the start. Right from seeing him in the yard that day. And seeing him on the beach. And hearing him. I was . . . lost in him."

"I thought you hated him."

"Thought I'd never get near him. Not with Ella around, then with you around."

"Me?"

"Yes, Claire. You. Why would he want a thing like me when he could have a girl like you?"

She swigged again.

"He was so beautiful," she whispered. "Wasn't he?"

"Yes."

"And the things he made you hear. And the things he made you feel."

"Yes, I know."

She screwed the cap back onto the bottle.

"I've been very drunk," she said. "But what I saw is true."

I waited again.

"It *was* love," she said. "Even if I didn't understand it myself till now. You don't go searching for somebody out of hate."

"You searched for him?"

"Yes. Just like I did on his wedding day. Leave home, travel North, find the bugger, flaunt yourself, offer yourself. I would've done anything. Anything."

She looked at me, as if she were a child, come here to be comforted.

"Oh hell, Claire," she said.

Her tears started to fall. I reached out to touch her. I went to the bed and sat with her and put my arm around her. She wept for a while.

"Oh, I'm so sorry," she said. "There was nothing I could do."

"Just tell me, Bianca."

She gathered her thoughts, her memories, then began.

"It was just me and Crystal. We hitchhiked. Dead easy. There was one bloke, all slimy and creepy in a shirt and tie that started getting ideas but Crystal give him one of her looks and he shut up. Dead easy. One lift then another, one lift then another. We weren't even sure where we were headin' and neither of us said what we were lookin' for. We were just shovin' off from school, from Krakatoa, from all of you lot. Couple of hours and there we were, early afternoon, walkin' through Alnmouth to the beach, eatin' ice-cream and giggling about what we'd left behind, but we both know we're lookin' out for him all the time. The beach is lovely, perfect warm white sand. Sea goin' on forever and the dunes stretchin' on forever. The castles on their rocks and the islands on the sea. I know you think I'm stupid and mebbe I am, but I'm clever enough to know we're blessed to be here, in this world. We don't need poets to tell us that. We walk. We hoy our shoes off and walk on the sand and in the water. Freedom. We've got a little tent and we've got scran and booze and fags, everything we need. Bliddy freedom! We dance and splash and yell about school and damn exams and the seagulls whoop above our heads. Ha! Then there he is."

She took another swig of vodka. She sat up straight, as if she was strengthening herself for what she had to say. I sat apart from her again.

"Orpheus?" I said.

"Aye. It was crazy. Like he'd put himself exactly where we'd find him, like he was waitin' or something, like we couldn't have come to any other place but this. There he is, singin', playin'. He's round that curve in the beach where them ancient timber shacks are. You know the ones? Must've been there since the year dot or before. He looks the same, mebbe a bit more haggard, a bit more frail. Crystal gasps. The teaser! she says. He was so damn gorgeous, Claire. And the voice. We couldn't move. Come and get me, Orpheus, I was beggin' inside myself.

Fat chance. There was others with him. All lads, it's right. They turn to us when we appear. I remember what James said about the blokes but I think sod them and I keep on walking closer. He stops singin'. He looks at us, like he's wary, like he's scared. One bloke plants hisself in front of us. 'You know us, Orpheus,' I go. 'We knew Ella. We know Claire.' Like a stupid thing I put me hands on me tits, like that'll help him to remember. 'Let them through,' he says, so mebbe the tit thing did work, eh? They let us sit with them. The blokes have got fruit and bread and stuff. They don't want our drink, don't want our fags. 'Where you been?' I ask, and Orpheus laughs. 'You should be at school,' he says, and it sounds so bliddy weird to be there with him and to hear that. 'We're havin' a few days of freedom,' says Crystal. 'Like you,' she says, and he just laughs at her, and plays again, and nobody wants to talk, and it's like there's nowt happenin', just the sun startin' to fall and the tide goin' out, and if it was anybody but him we'd have nicked off straight away, but we sat there and we watched him and we listened to him and all the time that thing inside is beggin', 'Take me, Orpheus. Take me now.' We should've left. Should've got out of it. It's the late afternoon when they arrive."

She swigged again.

"Who?" I said.

She looked away.

"Hell, Claire," she whispered. "Who knows? Was like they come out of the sea, out of the bliddy earth itself, out of the bliddy air, the light. One minute there's nobody, next minute they're dead close, already heading from the edge of the sea at us, already bliddy at us. Jesus Christ I think I'm hard. You should have had a look at them. Devils, maniacs. They're women, you know that from the hips and tits. Scars on them, tattoos, and wide wild eyes, like they've been snortin' something, like they're manic. And there's knives and hatchets and bliddy saws. And the nails on them, like claws, needles, daggers. Claire, he touches me. Orpheus *touches* me. 'Go away, Bianca,' he says. *Bianca*. 'Please run away,' he says. They hear him. 'He's right!' one screams. 'This is nowt to do with you.' Weird screamy voice, weird bliddy accent. Crystal's draggin' me. 'Come on, Bianca! Howay!' They're comin' closer. A couple of the blokes are running now. The others are backin' away. One stands in their path and gets a knife in his arm. 'Begone!' she screams again. 'We're doin' this for you, for all us bints. What's he turned from women for? Aye, Orpheus, what you turned from women for?' He stands up with the lyre and the women start to scream and howl and yell. 'We cannot hear you!' they scream. They yell louder, louder, come closer, closer. It's like they've known him forever, hated him forever, like they've been huntin' the earth for him forever. It was like this is how it was always meant to be and as if he knew that this was how it was always meant to be. Oh Jesus Christ how hard am I? He pushes me. 'Just go!' he says. And I see in his eyes that he cares for me, that he cares for all of us. And I love him. I bliddy love him love him love him, but all the same I want to run away with Crystal to the dunes. Ha! So much for how Love conquers Death. We don't get the chance to run. The yelling and screamin' gets louder. Two of the women get us in their claws. 'Sleep!' they hiss, and they spit something in our eyes. They kiss us and spit something in our mouths. They drop us to the sand and we're gone."

She paused.

"How can I get it out?" she said. "Will telling it help it to seem better? Will it seem more sane?"

She swigged the vodka.

"They killed him," I said.

"How did all this happen to us, Claire? We're just kids. We're just us. We're just . . ."

"They killed him."

"I seen some of it, but it was like dreams. I wondered

was I dyin' or already dead. We were drugged or something, out of it. I seen the knives and the hatchets goin' down. It was that wild at first. Screaming and yelling and thumpin' and rocks bangin'. The women crawling all around him and all over him. The fading light then a fire burnin'. Then the night with the stars shinin' down and it went all calm. Just little bursts of laughter from the women, just sighs and groans. Just the noise of the sea. And the night goin' on and goin' on and me and Crystal couldn't move. And I kept on thinkin', This is it. I'm dead."

She let a few tears fall. I reached out and touched her again, and she looked straight at me, biting her lips like a little girl.

"And the light come back," she said, "and I wished it hadn't. I wished that light would never come again. I wished that I'd been right when I thought that I was dead. I come out of the drugs or whatever it was. The women were still there. There was blood all over them. I'm tryin' to get up. One of them turns to me. 'We done this for you,' she said. 'Me?' I gasped. 'Aye. For all bints, always and everywhere. He's the cheater, he's the teaser. We done it for Ella.' 'For Ella?' I get up onto me elbows and I start to see. 'Aye,' she says. 'For her. He charmed her, he enticed her with his lalalalabliddyla. Charmer, teaser. And then he let her die.' I knelt up. She stood aside. 'And now,' she said, 'we've made him follow her.' And I saw him then, Orpheus, all in pieces, scattered on the sand, bits of him turnin' at the water's edge. Fingers, feet, bones, bits of him like joints of meat. His head in a rock pool further down and the lyre lyin' right beside it. Crystal's gaggin' and retchin'. And the women walk away, laughin'. 'He knew he had it comin'!' one of them yells. Mebbe I'm still half-drugged. There's spray above the sea, sand blowin' in the breeze and all that dazzling light from the risin' sun. The women are gone, quick as they came, and there's just me and Crystal and poor Orpheus and what the hell could we do, Claire? We back away like bairns. We see the crows droppin' down to him and jabbin' their beaks at him. We see things crawl out the sea to get bits of him. We see a big black dog running along the beach to get bits of him. And the sun's risin' and the sea's turnin' harder like it wants to get at him and carry more of him away. We see his head and his lyre lifted and carried out, Claire. We see what must be heart, liver, lungs. And the crows and gulls is goin' crazy for him. And here come more damn dogs. Oh, Claire, we couldn't run. We couldn't do nothin'. We stood in the dunes and saw Orpheus, all the bits of him, taken away. And the sea was so damn black like his blood had darkened it, and it came so bliddy high to clean away all sight of him. How long did we stay there? Who knows? Till afternoon, mebbe, and not a soul passed by, till there was just the beach, nothin' but the beach, and no more Orpheus nowhere to be seen."

She stared into the corner of the room, as if that was the sea, that was the beach.

"I saw it," she said at last. "But how can I believe it?"

"I don't know, Bianca."

"Crystal says it was all tricks and drugs and vodka. Must've been, she says. But it can't have been, can it?"

"I don't know, Bianca."

"And I know I'll keep on seeing it all me life and getting horrified by it."

She held her hands out to me and I took them and drew her closer. She rocked against me for a while.

"But it's weird," she said.

"What is?"

"It's like tellin' it helps it. And when I tell it, it's like, underneath it all, is a thing about love."

"Love?"

"I loved him and always loved him and always will."

She leaned close against me now. I held her gently.

"And it's like he loves me. Me, stupid thick Bianca. And like he loved all of us. He hardly saw us, he only saw Ella, and he loved her all the way to Death. But he loved us all, Claire. Is that stupid?"

"I don't know. I don't think so."

"He sang for us and played for us and made us feel . . . But there's no words for what he made us feel."

She rubbed the stains on her hands. Orpheus' blood crumbled from her skin.

"He was something, eh?" she whispered.

"Aye."

"He was bliddy something, and he came to us."

She kissed me on the cheek.

"I'm happy," she said. "Can that be right? That's the weirdest thing right now. I'm bliddy happy, Claire. How can that be?"

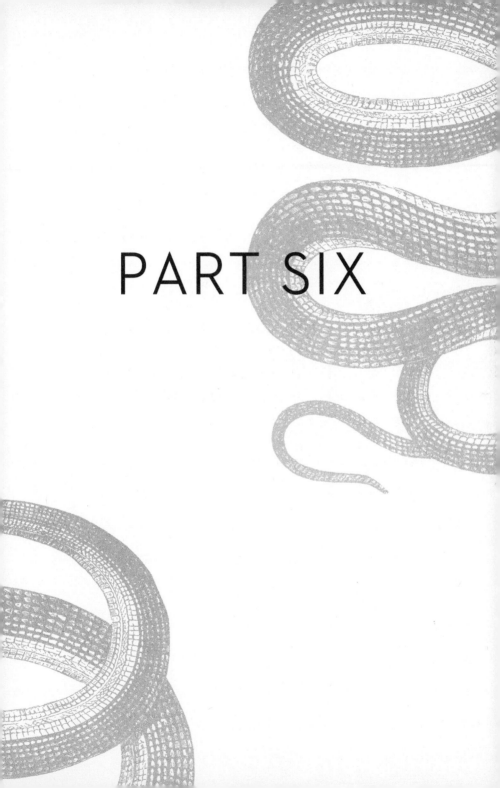

PART SIX

The night's gone. The sun's come up. The story's done.

Orpheus is with Ella again, wherever Death is, somewhere far beyond the Ouseburn gates. The rest of us go on. We continued with our lessons, our gatherings at The Cluny.

We did our exams in a weird state of ecstasy and distress.

I did well, of course.

"I'm so pleased, Claire," Krakatoa purred to me. "I always knew you had it in you."

I'm going south, to university, to read the words that make the world.

I already plan that next year I'll walk on the beaches of Greece. I'll drink ouzo and retsina with a still-to-be-encountered love. I'll feel sun that has true heat in it, swim in sea that isn't icy. I'll travel to the places where the ancient stories have their start.

I leave in just a few days' time. In the evenings, I sit longer than usual with my parents as we prepare to part. We look at old photographs: me as a baby, me as an infant, me as an adolescent, the three of us in beautiful formations in the world's shadows and light. We talk of the days before I was here, the day of my birth, the days of my growth. We laugh, we hug, we blink the tears from our eyes. We are members of a little family in a little home. Beyond us is Tyneside, the beaches and coalfields of Northumberland, the world, the galaxy, the universe, everything that there has ever been and will ever be.

I pack cases, gather clothes and belongings, things I need, things that I can't do without. Clothes, books, cash, credit card, some childhood toys. I'll take this earring as well. I found it yesterday. I went down to the Ouseburn to say farewell to the childhood monsters just beyond the gates. There it was, caught in the litter gathered at the base of the humming metal bars. I stretched down, teased it out, held it on my open palm. It's a little white dolphin earring. The gift of Ella, sent from Death.

Can that be true?

Yes. No. Maybe.

Maybe it's all been just coincidence, tale-telling,

rumour, madness, the madness of being young, the madness of knowing love for the first time, the madness of being alive in this miraculous place. Maybe we didn't really hear what we thought we heard, or we didn't hear it in the way we thought we heard. Maybe we didn't really see. Maybe we didn't feel what we thought we felt. Maybe . . .

But we did. We know we did.

And I know that he is gone and is still here.

I know that both of them are dead and both are young.

I hear him. His song is everywhere, is scattered like his flesh. He sings through beaks. He bleats with the lamb and howls with the wolf. He sings with the breeze through the treetops and the grass. He sings the petals of daisies, the berries of hawthorn, the taste of pears. He sings these bright late butterflies, and the dark new chrysalis where the butterfly will grow again. He sings the geese's glorious v-shaped migration and return. He sings the rays of the sun, the falling of the rain, the running of all water through Northumberland and the endless flowing of the Tyne. He sings us, us, us. He sings our flesh, our blood, our bones and breath. He comes and goes. Sometimes he stands at the edge of things, waiting for his chance to enter the world again. If we open ourselves to him and allow him into us, he will make us free. He will give us his song and let us dance.

I'll take the mask of Orpheus with me.

I'll keep it always.

I put it on now, the final act of telling this tale all night.

I look through his eyes. I breathe his breath.

Sing through me, Orpheus, as I speak these last words.

This word then this word then this then this.

Lose yourself, Claire.

Be gone. Be gone.

Be nothing.

And oh! He comes!

He comes, singing his way to my mouth, and there, just behind him, is beautiful beloved Ella, coming out from Death.